Holiday Heartstrings

Lauren Greene

To anyone who comfort watches *The Office* on repeat dreaming of a love
like Jim and Pam
You're not alone

Content Warning

Holiday Heartstrings includes mention of death of a parent due to cancer and scenes of expressed grief. I understand how hard it is to read about such matters, especially around the holiday's, so please read with care.

There is mention of cheating and explicit content on page as well.

Hugs,

Lauren

You are invited to

Christmas
Party

Friday, December 23rd

06.00 PM

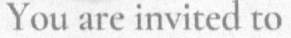

The Ridge Banquet Room

Greyridge, PA

RSVP to Paula in Reservations

Secret Santa Exchange-Dinner-Drinks

Penny,

I'm your Secret Santa. To be honest, I rigged the system a little. Taking Gary to a basketball game was quite the experience, but that story will have to wait.

This story is about you.

Take a look inside the bag. You'll find a roadmap of the memories we've made. Each item reminds me of you. The way you laugh. The way you narrow your eyes when you're mad. The way your entire face lights up when you grace the world with a genuine smile. Moments that were so small in the grand scheme of life, but, because of you, will always be special to me. You're so much more than a receptionist, Burke. And you're more than Scooter's fiancée or even my best friend.

You are everything.

Merry Christmas,

Jamie

Chapter One

DECEMER 22ND

"Because Christmas is the time to tell people how you feel."

I wiped my eyes on the nearest thing I could find, my elf puppy throw blanket. No matter how many times I'd watched it, this Christmas episode always got me.

The familiar clomp of my fiancé's boots at the back door caught my attention. He favored his right leg more when his knee was acting up. "Babe, is there still some dinner left?" he yelled in lieu of a greeting.

"There's some leftover soup in the fridge."

Me, soup, and *The Office*. I'm a party animal. Not that Scooter invited me out, but if he did, I would have opted out anyway. I preferred being warm and cozy by the twinkling lights that were wrapped around the mantle with my mistletoe candle burning.

Scooter leaned against the back of the couch and patted the top of my head. I hated it when he did that, but there was no reason to make a fuss.

"This show again? I don't know how you can stand to watch it as much as you do." He turned toward the kitchen and, like clockwork, I heard the crack of a beer can opening. "It's not even funny."

"I don't know. I just like it I guess." I watched him open and close the pantry a few times before sighing and returning behind the couch.

"I'm just going to pass out. I had some wings at Hooters with the guys, so I'll live. Plus, the cold is making my knee hurt like hell."

"Oh no. I'll be in soon," I said searching my mind for a different response but coming up empty.

He put his nearly empty can down on the end table, and I watched him head to our bedroom, scratching his ass as he went.

The episode rolled on with Michael acting like a tool, Angela angrily spiraling, and Pam realizing she had gotten the right gift after all. I pulled my blanket up to my chin and took comfort in the familiar storyline. I needed comfort this time of year.

This year especially.

"Hey Pen," Scooter called from our bedroom. I paused my show so I could hear him better. "My mom called earlier. She's going to come by the hotel tomorrow."

I sighed. My soon-to-be mother-in-law was hell-bent on driving me insane. "Did she say why?"

He came out and leaned on the doorframe in nothing but his tighty-whities. The Scooter I met when I was seventeen was nowhere to be found now at 28. I didn't mind his expanded belly or prematurely thinning hairline, but sometimes it was hard to believe he had been one of the hottest guys I'd ever met.

"How should I know? Wedding crap." He grunted and scratched his chin. "You know I'm too busy for this shit, Pen. You need to deal with her."

My face fell at his sharpness. He must have noticed because he came to sit beside me.

"I'm sorry if I'm acting like an asshole. The hotel is busy, and a bunch of my guys are on vacation. I don't have time for wedding nonsense. I work hard. Maybe I'm hungry. You can't expect me to eat soup for dinner. You know?"

He pecked me on the cheek as I nodded. "I'll see what she needs tomorrow. Hopefully, she'll come when I can take a quick break."

"That's my girl."

I forced my lips into a smile.

"I know a way you can make me feel better," he said, his voice low. He reached across my shoulders and rubbed his calloused fingers along my upper arm. "Why don't you turn off this garbage and come to bed? We only have a few days before you're my wife. And if my cousin's honest, the second him and Trisha got married, it was like she had a padlock between her legs."

I couldn't blame Trisha. Russell was the worst. I forced a laugh anyway.

"You're not going to do that to me are you, Pen?" He rested a palm on my thigh and squeezed gently before creeping the tips of his fingers to the waistband of my pajama pants. I shook my head and let him pull me into the bedroom where he wasted no time in stripping down and climbing on top of me.

As I laid there, staring at the ceiling and letting out well-timed moans. I couldn't help but let my mind wander to how I'd gotten here.

"Hey Penny, are those elf ears regulation size? They look smaller than they should."

"They're the ones you provided me, Mr. Holliday." I glanced down at my hideously green elf dress and candy cane striped tights. "The whole uniform is what you gave me."

My boss huffed. It was a sound so in contrast with the way he was dressed that I almost laughed. How did he expect me to take him seriously when I was dressed as an elf, and he was wearing a light-up blazer decorated with reindeer?

He must have seen me smirking because he narrowed his eyes and pointed to the kiosk where I was supposed to be checking in guests for their photos with Santa.

If you asked me a few months ago if I wanted my first high school job to be working the mall Christmas Town display as an elf, I would have given an enthusiastic yes. I loved Christmas. The decorations, the music, the hope, and the memories that were made every day for a whole month.

Unfortunately, I had failed to consider the fact that my boss would be the biggest Grinch in all of Greyridge. That and maybe I wasn't cut out to work with screaming toddlers and stressed-out mothers after I'd been at school all day.

The line was ten people deep and the CD we played on repeat had already cycled three times. It should be a crime to listen to The Jackson 5 Christmas Album that many times. That was when I felt a tap on my shoulder. I spun around, my face most definitely not looking the part of a cheery North Pole helper, and I came face to face with a chest. A guy's chest. And he was also dressed as an elf. I craned my neck, eyes widening.

"Scooter Anderson? Wh-why are you wearing that?" I stammered, trying to wrap my mind around the image of the star quarterback of my school's football team tapping my shoulder, dressed in tights.

"It's my first shift." He adjusted his pointy hat and lowered his gaze to my feet. "The guy in the crazy jacket said I should come talk to you."

"Oh. Okay..." I took another look at the line of impatient families and then back toward Santa aka Bob, who was waiting for me to usher the next kiddo over to him. I had been doing it all the whole week—taking photos, line management, cash register. I'd barely had time to eat a candy cane, so help was much needed. "Why don't you work on line management, and I'll focus on taking photos and working the register. I can teach you how to do that stuff as we go."

He met my gaze, then flashed a smile that rendered me speechless. I could see why all the girls crushed on him even if he was more brawn than brains. Seeing a six-foot-tall football player in tights and a ruffled shirt made even Scooter Anderson seem as intimidating as a kitten.

He nodded, then groaned. "Oh shit." His eyes widened. "I can't let them see me."

"Who?" I looked around. "What's wrong?"

"Excuse me. We've been waiting here for a half hour. We want Santa!" an angry woman in line yelled over the seventies holiday tunes.

Before I knew what was happening, Scooter wrapped his arms around me and kissed me. It was my first kiss, so I had nothing to compare it to. But, in my mind, the twinkle lights glowed brighter and the Jackson 5 suddenly sounded like angels singing. My skin lit up beneath his grip and thought left my brain. His warm breath floated up my nostrils, smelling like a cross between pizza and mints. Teenage me reveled in it.

His mouth stilled, and I opened my eyes to see him searching the area while pressed against me. Sighing, he moved me to arm's length.

"You saved me. I'd never hear the end of it if the guys saw me dressed like this." He rubbed his lips with the back of his hand.

Rendered speechless, I leaned on one foot with my mouth slightly open. "Wait what?"

"I couldn't let them see me here. I had to hide. Thanks for helping me out." He flashed another grin, and I nodded like an idiot.

"I'm going to get back to work now. Thank y-you," I stuttered. "Not thank you for kissing me just thanks for...um... never mind." I had no clue what nonsense I was uttering. He smiled again with his brow raised and then went to smooth over the angry moms.

He ended up asking me out for hot chocolate at the drive-through, of course, after his first shift. God forbid he risked being seen in his work uniform. The entire month we worked together, I had to "help hide him" quite a few times. Sometimes multiple times a day. I didn't mind. Yet a tiny part of me wondered why he couldn't be honest with his buddies.

And that's how we started dating ten years ago. The quiet bookworm and the popular jock. Typical small town love story. Only, by the following Christmas my life changed forever and my love story became one of heartache and grief.

Scooter rolled over in his sleep, pulling most of the comforter with him. I wasn't tired. Plus, I wanted to finish my episode. I loved the ending when everyone winds up having a great time and they leave the office together. With only a few days until Christmas, I wanted to soak up any small amount of comfort I could.

It was late, but I knew Jamie would be up. He was a night owl too.

> **Me:** *I'm on my 4th rewatch of Christmas Party. Bet I have you beat.*

I waited a few minutes, then pattered into the kitchen to make a cup of Sleepytime tea. My phone buzzed, and I wasted no time sliding the screen open.

> **Jamie:** *4th? Amateur numbers, Burke.*

> **Me:** *That's only this year. I have watched it at least 20 times total.*

A grin spread across my face.

Jamie: *20 is respectable. I don't think I want to tell you my number.*

Jamie: *I'll seem pathetic now that I think about it.*

Me: *Nope. Spill it, Hart.*

Jamie: *8 times this month alone and that's just the Christmas Party episode.*

Jamie: *I've had all the holiday episodes on repeat.*

Me: *Wow...*

Me: *I better get caught up.*

Jamie: *Slacker*

Jamie: *:)*

I chuckled then brought my favorite World's Best Boss mug to my lips to blow the steam away.

Me: *See you in the morning...*

Jamie: *Night, Burke*

Two episodes later, I curled into my side of the bed and yanked a sliver of blanket from Scooter's comatose body. Scrolling to my wedding count-down app, I checked off another day. Only three more nights until I could call myself Mrs. Anderson. I listened to him let out a part grunt, part snore and sighed. I was a lucky woman...

Penny,

Remember the first time we met? I've never admitted this to you, but I remember every single second of that moment like it was yesterday. Maybe it's cheesy, but when I saw you standing behind the front desk, it was like the world around me blurred, and all I could focus on was your face.

I already felt out of sorts about starting a new job in a new town since I up and moved from Connecticut when my brother needed me. Then Gary, being Gary, made me wear one of those neon yellow nametag stickers on my jacket. It felt like I had a spotlight following me as he gave me a tour of the office. After he brought me around the back offices, barging into not one, but three, meetings, we came out to the lobby.

To you.

Like I said above, Burke, I saw you and everything stood still. Your hair was extra curly that day, probably because of the early summer humidity. You had it up in a clip with little pieces framing your face. The closer I got, the more I noticed the sprinkle of freckles around the bridge of your nose, your creamy skin and the thick dark lashes framing your incredible green eyes. Then you smiled, and I think my heart stopped.

You probably thought I was a creep gawking at you like that. You've never said anything, but I've always wondered what your first impression of me was.

Then you saw the name tag and laughed.

You told me yours was bright green when you started. When you grabbed a marker and took a few steps toward me, I think I held my breath the entire time. You uncapped the marker and wrote something under my name.

Newbie.

Just like someone from sales had done to you on your first day. You said I was initiated now, part of the family. Or at least that's what I think you said. The pounding of my pulse in my ears made it difficult to hear much of anything. When Gary pulled me away to go meet the bellmen, I knew I'd met the most incredible woman to live and breathe on this earth.

So, Burke, present number one, is my nametag. I took it off that night and stuck it to a sheet of paper to remember the first moment I met you.

Jamie

Chapter 2

DECEMBER 23RD

Scooter slid his truck into the employee parking lot across the street from The Ridge Hotel, narrowly avoiding a patch of black ice. It was seven in the morning, and no one had salted the ground yet. The picturesque hotel where we both worked stood out against a backdrop of pine forest and the snow-capped Moosic Mountains. I wished I could say I had the same enthusiasm about coming in to work that I had when I first started nine years ago, but I'd be lying.

The way we decorated every inch of the grounds in white lights and evergreen boughs with a ten-foot tree on each side of the glass entryway doors used to fill me with joy. Now it all served as a reminder that I could never escape Christmas tourists.

Scooter kissed my forehead and hurried ahead of me around back so he could clock in on time. He was the head of maintenance and surprisingly he cared about being there at the same time as his crew. He probably didn't know I knew that they spent the first hour sitting around drinking coffee and ignoring requests from the front of house.

"Bye, babe," he yelled over his shoulder. "Don't forget about my mom coming."

"Yup," I said under my breath. There was no use responding when he was already crossing the street.

I was running late, thanks to Scooter pressing snooze. I grabbed everything I needed from the backseat—my insulated lunch bag, purse, notebook, and wedding planning binder. Belongings in hand, I trekked across the lot toward the main entrance. An icy breeze swept by, and I cursed having to wear a skirt with sheer pantyhose instead of pants. It was two degrees. I'd like to see my boss in a skirt and see how long he'd last.

I trudged along so deep in thought that I didn't see the patch of black ice. My arms windmilled in slow motion, and I dropped everything. I braced myself, knowing it was going to hurt like hell.

"Whoa, Burke. Looks like you forgot your skates." A strong pair of hands caught me around the waist and held me upright. "I got you."

"Thanks." My breaths came out in hazy puffs. "That was not how I wanted to start today."

Jamie looked down at me with a flicker of amusement in his eyes. "I don't think anyone wants to start their day by cracking their head open, Burke." Then he laughed, a light sound that floated from his lips. I loved his laugh. It was one of the first things I noticed about him when we'd met five years ago.

"I guess you're right," I said, then bent to gather my things. Jamie crouched to pick up my notebook and wedding binder. He read the words across the front of the binder, and I swore I saw his face drop before he handed it over to me. "Thanks. I hope it didn't get all wet."

I brushed it off with my hand, the cool snow on it stinging. Jamie eyed my notebook like he was about to peek inside. I cleared my throat. "Ever heard of privacy, Hart?" I teased and held out my hand for it. He handed it over slowly but casually.

"Just seeing what the future bestselling author is working on today. Hold my hand. It's icy out here." He reached for my free hand, and I placed my palm in his, enjoying his warmth.

"Bestselling author in my dreams, you mean," I laughed. "I think you need to finish a book to become an author."

We walked carefully across the treacherous parking lot.

"I believe in you. What you've read to me is incredible. I'm dying for more, which is why I had to try and snag a tiny peek. Not to mention I'd get total brownie points with my niece if I gave her some spoilers."

"I still can't believe you showed her that chapter. It was totally unedited."

"Didn't matter to her. She's twelve and dragon obsessed so you're pretty much the coolest person in her eyes. I agree with her."

His compliment went in one ear and out the other. I never really knew how to take a compliment and he handed them out like free candy canes at Christmas. Regardless, I gave up on being an author a long time ago. But every once in a while, Jamie persuaded me to let him read some of my stuff on our lunch breaks. He was just being nice. I knew it wasn't any good. Plus, a guy like Jamie interested in YA fantasy? Doubtful.

"How are Jack and the kids doing, by the way? I saw him last time I went to grab a coffee and he looked overwhelmed." I glanced up at Jamie, hoping I wasn't prying. From what Jamie had told me about his brother over the years, I've surmised that Jack kept his personal life under wraps.

"Jack, overwhelmed? That doesn't surprise me in the least. He's as stubborn as they come and fights tooth and nail to let anyone help him. They're hanging in there though." He smiled a small lopsided grin that didn't quite reach his eyes as we approached the lobby entrance.

"After you," he said, holding open the door. Warm air and the smell of pine enveloped me. Jamie came behind the front desk with me and helped me plop all my belongings underneath it so they were out of the way.

"See you at lunch?" I asked. We always had lunch together. Scooter and I used to years ago, but he told me the guys needed him downstairs. Jamie held up his brown paper bag like a trophy.

"Me and my ham sandwich will see you at noon." He pushed his too-long hair out of his face and gave me a small wave before heading to the back offices where he worked in the sales department.

Guests trickled up to check out or asked for directions to local restaurants. I considered it a fairly quiet morning until Gary made his first of many walk-throughs of the lobby.

"Penny for your thoughts?" he asked, hiding his laughter behind his hand. I clicked away from the check-in screen and blinked at him. "Get it? Penny for your thoughts. Your name is Penny."

"Clever, Mr. Woods," I said.

"How goes the morning rush? Looks like you're working really hard on the old computer." He leaned a forearm on the granite front desk counter and tapped his finger while humming the tune of "The Little Drummer Boy." Amelia from housekeeping had just polished it to a shine, and he was leaving smudges.

"Everything's in order." Usually, if I answered in short sentences, he'd get bored and go bother someone else. How he had kept his position as general manager for over ten years was beyond me. He stood up to his full height and turned his head toward the back-office's entrance.

"Jameson Hart, the man, the myth, the legend. How's it hanging, my man? See the game last night?" Jamie peeked half his body through the doorway. I smirked at him in a silent thanks for refocusing our squirrely boss.

He cleared his throat, ignoring Gary, and held out a paper plate. "Penny, I snagged you a donut from the breakroom before Calvin sniffed them out."

"Boston cream?" I asked excitedly.

"Of course," he grinned.

"Yessss." I grabbed the plate and stuck it out of view of the guests. "You're the best."

His eyes lit up.

"If you two are done making googly eyes at each other, we have work to do," Gary said.

"Wha-we weren't," I stumbled. It was no use. As soon as the attention was off of him, he acted like a bored child.

"I wish we could skip to the party," Gary groaned. "It's going to be legendary. Epic. Talked about for centuries to come. You all set with your gifts?" he asked. "It is the most important day of the year."

"Right. The work Christmas party is the most important day of the year. Even more important than my Christmas wedding," I deadpanned.

"That's why I hired you, Burke. You know where your priorities are. What about you, good sir?" he focused back on Jamie. "You ready to par-tay?"

Jamie saluted him. "Yup. Can't wait."

"Very good. Remember to get all your work done early. I wouldn't want you to miss the festivities," he chided.

Jamie clicked his tongue. "Will do, boss man. See you later, Penny."

When Gary finally got distracted by a delivery that came in through the wrong door, I sighed a breath of relief. Hopefully, he'd get pulled back to his office to do actual work or at least not linger in the lobby all day.

A chill crept up my back. I thought it was from the lobby door being propped open, but I should have known better. Her signature Chanel No. 5 wafted toward me from ten feet away, and her heels clicked along the Italian marble floors.

Barbara Anderson. My soon-to-be mother-in-law.

It's not that I hated the woman. We'd had a few nice moments together in the past ten years, like the time she almost complimented my deviled eggs at Easter brunch. She did move them off the dining table and into the kitchen, but she had muttered that they were delightful. There was also last year when she decided to include me in the family Christmas gift exchange. It only took nine years of being with her son to earn that privilege. I'd gotten a new mop, but at least she had thought of me.

Okay. Who was I kidding? I loathed her.

She walked toward me with her upper lip already curled.

"Penny," she said in lieu of a greeting, then plucked a piece of invisible lint from her shoulder. "I'll meet you by the fireplace so we can go over some changes."

Of course she hadn't asked if I could take a break. I bit my inner cheek. Something I did every time I had to be in the same breathing space as her, so seeing as my wedding was in a few days and she'd taken control of the planning, my mouth had more than a few sore spots.

After I peeked my head in the back for front desk coverage, I joined her at one of the lobby's leather couches. She already had a few sheets of cardstock spread out along the coffee table as well as an iPad open to the app she'd been using to stay organized.

"After careful consideration, I'd like to move your side of the family here." She pointed to a circle on our seating chart that was far away from the bridal table. "Since you only have five relatives coming, there's no sense wasting a whole table of eight near the head of the room."

I blinked, letting her words sink in. She wanted to move my only family members as far away from me as possible? My father would be sitting in the back of the banquet room near the restrooms?

"That-that's not okay." I inhaled through my nose wishing her perfume would evaporate.

"Not okay?"

Nodding, I repeated myself. "I want my family near me on my wedding day."

Without meeting my eyes, she shuffled papers around and mumbled to herself.

"I've already changed the chart and sent it to my coordinator." She tapped a manicured nail on the iPad screen. "I had no idea this would be an issue, Penny. I took time out of my day to show you so there'd be no mistakes this weekend. I wouldn't want Scooter to be upset on his big day."

I forced myself to study the vase of flowers across the room with its intricate pattern and full petals. My eyes did that thing where they only half focused, and for a second, it was almost like I was somewhere else, somewhere without the devil incarnate sitting beside me. I bit the same spot in my cheek again, wincing.

"*His* big day?" My voice wasn't my own. It drifted in from far away.

"Of course. Scooter Senior and I wouldn't be funding the whole thing if it wasn't his special day. I cannot wait to be a grandmother. I hope you're not planning to wait much longer." She reached out to touch the outer corner of my eye. "Those crow's feet tell me you don't have many years left. I'm sure it's from working here for so long, but soon you can take your place at home."

I closed my eyes. Had she really said that? Like to my face? My ears started to burn.

"What am I missing over here? Hope you're not having too much fun without me?"

Blinking, I turned my head toward the voice I knew so well. The voice that belonged to the one person who could always put a smile on my face.

"Hello, Jameson," Barbara said. "You're looking well."

Barbara made eyes at him. You'd never catch her treating a man in a suit disrespectfully, especially a younger, handsome man. She was more of a misogynist than most men I knew.

"Penny, sorry to interrupt, but you're needed in the back offices for a meeting," he said matter-of-factly. Barbara fixed her gaze back on her pile of notes, and he winked at me.

"Oh," I feigned dismay. "Looks like we'll have to finish this discussion another time."

Sorting everything back into her handbag, she stood up. "I suppose. Have Cootie give me a call when he gets home. I know he's terribly busy managing so many employees and all, but he never makes time for his mother."

Jamie mouthed, "Cootie?" at me, and I bit back laughter.

"I will, goodbye."

I speed walked behind Jamie as fast as I could across the lobby without busting my tail on the marble. "In here," he said, pulling me into the nearest refuge—the coat closet.

We sidestepped wrapped Christmas presents, shopping bags, and an entire box of guest welcome bags until we reached the back of the small space.

"You," I said between pants, "are my savior." I sagged against a puffy ski jacket and rubbed my temples. "I can't stand that woman. I honestly wonder if she's even a real person."

Jamie chuckled, warm and deep. "You think she's some sort of alien?"

"A Stepford wife for sure," I said.

Jamie rubbed the back of his neck and leaned against the wall opposite me. The gold flecks in his hazel eyes seemed to shine in the semi-darkness.

"It's hard to believe that I'm going to have to deal with her for the rest of my life."

He stayed quiet but kept pulling on the back of his neck. The silence became too loud.

"I mean, she's a nightmare, am I right?" I chuckled. "The coast is probably clear now. So," I reached out and gave his shoulder a light punch, "thanks for coming to my rescue. I, uh, I'll deal with the whole seating chart mess later." I was about to pull my hand away but he pressed his palm against mine and held steady. My breath hitched. "Jamie?"

Dropping his palm to his side and rubbing it against his pant leg he said, "You're welcome."

"I should go," I said quickly before I slipped out the door and back behind my desk without glancing over my shoulder.

Penny,

Present number two is one you may scratch your head looking at. I know a napkin isn't a great gift. But that napkin has a story behind it.

The first time we had lunch together was a few weeks after I started. It had taken me that long to work up the nerve to talk to you. Pathetic, right? But every time I saw you, I clammed up. And you really didn't want to see me stuttering on my words, trust me.

It happened to be employee appreciation day. And, as you know, one of Gary's redeeming qualities as a boss is his fondness for buying us enormous amounts of food. I was stuck on a call for over an hour and missed lunch. If I could somehow find that guest and thank her for booking a twenty-room block at precisely that time, I'd hug her tight because when I finally made it into the break room, there you were. You had missed lunch too.

I almost turned around and jogged back to my office, but I took a deep breath, checked that I wasn't a sweaty mess, and walked in beside you. We joked about how Gary had ordered bologna because, seriously, who even eats that stuff? Then we ended up making Frankenstein monster versions of sandwiches by assembling an edible meal with parts of the leftovers.

You made me feel comfortable enough to joke. It was easy. Not only were you gorgeous but talking to you was like climbing a massive tree. I wanted to get to the top, see the incredible view, but also enjoy every step I had to take to get there. I wanted to feel each branch under my fingertips, trace their ridges, learn the patterns of your leaves, peel away the bark and see what lay underneath.

When we parted ways, I felt hopeful for the first time in a long time, so I kept one of our napkins. Don't worry, it's unused. There are no ancient bologna stains on it or anything. It's just a small memento from the best lunch I've ever had.

-Jamie

Chapter 3

DECEMBER 23RD

When Emmy came at lunchtime for her shift, I almost bear hugged her. I was so ready to take a break, mostly from the lobby holiday music station that repeated the same carols every hour, or maybe those were just the ones that crept into my brain like the earworms they were.

Only one more day left I told myself, then I'd be off for my wedding and honeymoon. By the time I'd get back, no more carols. The boring elevator music we played eleven months of the year didn't torture me nearly as much. I grabbed my notebook and wedding binder and made my way through the back offices and into the employee break room.

"There she is, the bride-to-be." Paula, the sweet reservations supervisor, crooned before I even had a chance to sit down. She put her knitting project down on the table. "You must be so excited after waiting so many years for this. How many was it again? Seven?"

"Eight," I winced. It had been eight years since Scooter proposed. I tried not to think about how young I was. How I was nineteen and newly engaged when my life was in complete shambles. I remember looking at the ring, a gaudy family heirloom, in his outstretched hand and thinking at least I wouldn't be alone.

"It'll be worth the wait...," her voice trailed off. "A day to remember."

She went back to her knitting, done with the conversation. Jamie came in behind me and placed his palm at the small of my back, sending a shiver up my spine. "Ready to eat? I brought you something. Let's call it an early Christmas party treat."

"You did?" I perked up. "You didn't have to do that."

We sat at our usual round table. I unwrapped my turkey sandwich and took a bite while Jamie pulled out his food. Always the same, a ham sandwich on wheat bread, a Ziploc bag of baby carrots, and water. I'd teased him for years for being so boring, but he's always told me he liked the predictability of it. It made him feel good to know there was at least one constant in his days. Who was I to argue when that made all kinds of sense. The break room was no frills compared to the rest of the hotel. It had fluorescent lighting, cracked vinyl tile flooring, and plastic chairs. Jamie and I joked that law enforcement interrogation rooms looked more comfortable.

"You ready for the party later?" he asked as he cracked open his water.

"You mean the most important day of the year according to Gary? Of course I am. Got my outfit picked out, Secret Santa present wrapped, and best of all... Scooter promised to be the designated driver this year. What about you?"

He wiped a drop of water from the corner of his mouth and sat back. "I was born ready. Want to bet on how long it'll take Gary to ruin the night? I'm thinking... fifteen minutes."

"Only fifteen minutes? Wow, so little faith in him." I laughed and then sipped my iced tea.

"My bet is well thought out and centered around five years of historical accuracy. I stand by it." His playful tone continued. "I think it was the party three years ago where he outed a guy from maintenance for cheating on his wife in the first ten minutes, right?"

I groaned. "I forgot about that. Poor Tessa left in tears when Gary called her the wrong name. She was already suspicious about who Isaac was cheating with." I opened my bag of grapes and popped one into my mouth. "Maybe you're right. I'm trying to be optimistic though."

"What's your guess?" he asked, brow raised.

"I say an hour. Hopefully, he doesn't ruin things before we get to eat." The party was taking place in the banquet room of the hotel's adjoining restaurant. I was looking forward to the buffet. They made the best pasta primavera I'd ever had.

Jamie reached his hand out to shake on our bet. "Don't leave me hanging." I wrapped my hand around his, shaking in a business-like manner before a laugh slipped out.

We ate more of our lunch and fell into companionable silence. I opened my wedding binder to look at the seating chart my evil mother-in-law wanted to mess with. There was no reason for her to do what she was doing at this point. We were a few days away, and everything was done. The only part left was to say I do.

Jamie didn't ask about the wedding plans, and I didn't offer up details. Anytime he saw me doing wedding stuff, he got weirdly quiet. He was probably not interested, and I didn't blame him. Wedding planning was bad enough when you were the bride, if I didn't have to deal with it, I certainly wouldn't.

When our hour dwindled and we finished our lunches, he rested his forearms on the table. His button up's sleeves were rolled up, and I focused on his exposed lean muscles. Why were forearms so attractive?

"You forgot your present," he said and rubbed his palms together while waiting for my reply.

"I didn't forget," I said quietly. "It's rude to bring up something like that."

"Nothing you could ever say to me would be rude, Burke." I worried my lip, trying to avoid biting my inner cheek again. He sounded so serious, so sincere. "You can ask me anything. Okay?"

His hazel eyes drew me in, and my stomach flipped. I nodded, smiling softly. He reached into his lunch bag and pulled out a small container. When I saw what was inside, I couldn't hold back my grin.

Inside the container was Jamie's famous Everything Bars of Randomness. We'd aptly named them over text one night a few years ago. He was staying with his parents over a long holiday weekend and was so bored he decided to attempt baking something. He dug through his mother's baking shelf in the pantry and threw in anything and everything he found. He sent me pictures the entire time, and I swore they'd be the most disgusting things ever created. But to both of our surprise, when he brought them in to work a couple of days later, they tasted incredible. Maybe it was the coconut mixed with the pistachios and white chocolate chips, or maybe it was the crushed cookie and the cinnamon. We didn't know the magic behind the bars, only that they were one of a kind and sacred.

"You baked them again?" I asked excitedly.

With a childlike look in his eyes, he answered, "Last night. I wanted to surprise you."

My heart was going to burst. He uncovered the container, took out a crumbly piece, and handed it to me. I closed my eyes and took a bite, savoring the mix of flavors and textures on my tongue. A moan slipped out, and I opened my eyes to find Jamie's gaze fixed on my mouth.

He cleared his throat. "Are they as good as last time?"

I nodded and swallowed the bite. "Better. You've outdone yourself."

His whole face lit up. "I'm glad you like them." He slid the container across the table to me.

"Best present ever."

Back at the front desk, I settled in for the holiday weekend check-in rush. Nothing could spoil my mood after Jamie's present, not even looking at my screen and seeing that I'd likely be bombarded by stressed-out travelers any minute. After I put in a call to the restaurant to double check they'd be sending the correct number of welcome cookies over and helping a couple with directions to the nearest mall, I took a moment to breathe.

I pulled my phone out of my purse to see if I had any messages. Cellphones weren't exactly allowed behind the desk, but after nine years of working here, I'd never gotten in trouble for it. I always made sure the lobby was clear before taking the chance.

I had a missed call from my father shortly after I got back from lunch. Besides his missed call, the only other message was from Barbara. It was a two-word message that said New Chart and a photo. My jaw clenched as I swiped her message away, leaving it unanswered. Do not let the magic of the everything bars get squashed by her, I told myself.

Rubbing my temple, I clicked my father's name to call him back. I hadn't talked to him in a few days with all the stress of the wedding and Christmas. He answered on the second ring.

"Hey, angel, how's it going?" my dad's voice boomed. He was many things but quiet was not one of them.

"Hanging in there. At work getting ready for check-ins."

"Right. I won't keep you. Darlene and I can't wait for Sunday. You need any last-minute help with anything?" Darlene said something to him in the background. "Jason came in from the city for the weekend, so he can help too."

"Darlene must be happy to have her son home for the holiday," I said, resting my elbows against the counter.

"She is. They've been wrapping gifts and baking together. I think his boyfriend may join us on Sunday too. I figured you wouldn't mind giving Jason a last minute plus one?"

"That sounds so nice for them." My voice wavered as Christmas memories of my mom and I in the kitchen covered in flour popped into my mind. Ever since I could remember we made sugar cookies on Christmas Eve. They usually came out looking like demented blob versions of what we were aiming for, but nothing tasted sweeter.

"Angel? You still there?" Dad asked, breaking me from my thoughts.

"Yeah, sorry. A guest walked by." I trapped the phone against my shoulder. "What were you saying?"

"I was asking if you needed any help before Sunday?" he said.

"No, I have everything covered." I forced a smile hoping it would help my voice sound anything other than how I felt. "Thank you for the offer though. You should spend time with Darlene and Jason. I'm sure they'd like that."

"Why don't you drive up and join us tomorrow? We can have dinner and exchange gifts before the big day?" He softened his tone. "I know this time of year is difficult. It is for me too, angel." An invisible string pulled the muscles of my chest inward.

I forced a shaky breath, willing the emotions back down where they could stay buried. I didn't have it in me to dig up those feelings. Not today. "I'm fine, Dad, really. I wish I could join you guys, but we're going over to Scooter and Barbara's for Christmas Eve dinner. Thank you for the invite."

A flurry of movement outside the doors caught my eye. The rush was about to begin. Joy to the world.

"I have to go. Some guests are about to head inside. I'll see you on Sunday."

"Angel?" he asked.

"Yes?"

"It's okay to miss her." He sounded so soft and gentle, nothing like his normal booming tone. At that moment, all I wanted was to crawl through the phone and get wrapped up in his strong arms. "She's there with you. I know it."

A tear slipped out of the corner of my eye, and I rubbed it away. Taking another deep breath, I thanked my dad and hit end call. His words lingered at the back of my mind for the rest of the afternoon. If my mom was still here, would she be happy for me?

Penny,

Since we're on the topic of lunch, I have to say you've been the best lunch date I've ever had. You make sitting in a crappy breakroom eating a boring ham sandwich the highlight of my whole day. It's not only our lunches, but it's anytime we get to sneak a few minutes together to take a breather or have a cup of incredibly stale back-office coffee. There's been more than a few times when I'd already had a few cups but saw you head in there and made myself drink another just to be near you. Remember that time I accidentally made my cup with brown sugar instead of white? It's still a mystery who mixed those in there to begin with. The world may never know. I took one sip and almost spit it across the room, but you laughed so hard. God, you looked so beautiful when you laughed like that. Your whole body shook and tears sprang to your eyes, darkening your lashes even more.

You insisted on tasting the abomination and ended up loving it. Then I was the one laughing in disbelief. I've tried brown sugar in my coffee like three other times to be sure it wasn't a breakroom coffee thing... but nope, I couldn't do more than a sip.

Present number three is a packet of brown sugar.

A bonus present is a secret I've been keeping. It's me who's been restocking the brown sugar packets in the breakroom. You deserve all the sweetness you want.

-Jamie

Chapter 4

December 23rd

I only had one more hour left in my shift when Mrs. McCormick shuffled into the lobby. Her huge handbag swayed from her shoulder and our burly bellman, Chris, pulled a luggage cart full of packages behind her. He widened his eyes when they reached the desk.

What is it now, Universe?

"Hello, dear," she began. "I spoke to this nice man," she gestured to Chris, "and he told me you'd be able to help me mail these packages. You see, I need them to be sent by overnight mail to my grandchildren in Arizona."

My already tight chest muscles pulled taut. The post office on the last Friday before Christmas would be like walking into a disaster zone equal to post-tornado Kansas, especially since Greyridge's post office was the size of a closet and was run by a man who very well may have been older than Santa himself.

I was searching my brain for a reason to get out of this when Jamie pushed through the back-office door. I eyed him, trying to convey a silent help me. He took one look at Mrs. McCormick and then at the massive pile of packages behind her before realization shone on his face.

"Happy holidays. What can I help you with, ma'am?" He came up next to me at the counter and gave Mrs. McCormick a warm smile.

"I was explaining to this lovely woman that I need help mailing these gifts for my grandchildren. I have five. Let's see," she looked over at the pile, "these are for Jenny. She's my oldest. Then there's Thomas and Tanya, the twins. They just turned nine..."

If we didn't cut her off, we'd be sitting here until long after the post office closed. Maybe that was a good thing. I'd get out of this errand. But poor little Tommy and Tanya would be out what looked like a sweet haul.

"I'd love to hear all about your family, Mrs. McCormick, but if we are going to help you, we need to get these out right away." Jamie glanced at Chris. "Chris, can you take the van?"

Chris shook his head. "Can't. I have an airport pickup for a VIP and then Gary told me to take off early to get ready for tonight."

Jamie scrunched his brows. "Who else is on bell duty?"

His voice got low as he leaned closer to us. "Melvin. He was the only one who volunteered to work the late shift tonight. He said he didn't mind missing the party since he had his own party to go to tomorrow... at The White House..." Chris made a swirly gesture at his temple.

Jamie and I looked at each other and nodded. There was no way we could let Melvin handle this. Frankly, Melvin could barely handle holding the door open most days. He was entertaining though especially on slow days.

"Penny and I will take care of the packages, Mrs. McCormick. Don't you worry." Jamie reached under the desk and squeezed my palm as his way of apologizing for what he'd agreed to. My hand tingled at the contact, sending little sparks up the length of my arm.

We sent Mrs. McCormick on her way. While Jamie and Chris loaded Jamie's car with the packages, I waited for Emmy to get back from her break. We would be cutting it close on time, but hopefully, we'd make it. I wouldn't want to see that sweet woman upset if we missed.

Jamie's Civic was not built to haul packages. The entire backseat and trunk were packed tightly, but there was still room for me in the passenger seat thankfully. He had to pull his seat up an inch or two to fit everything into the backseat and somehow, I only just noticed how much longer his legs were than mine.

"I didn't get to thank you before," I said while Jamie navigated through town.

"For the bars? I'm pretty sure you already did."

"Not the bars." I fidgeted with the zipper on my coat. "For this. For helping me. I would have ended up doing this alone, which would have meant driving Scooter's truck, and he hates when I drive his truck."

He glanced at me with a distant expression before setting his sight back on the road. I felt the need to explain myself. We already stuffed the car full, which had left no room for awkward silences in the cracks between presents.

"It means a lot. To be able to count on someone...," I trailed off before I let any more humiliating thoughts slip out. Jamie was my closest friend, but there were some things I didn't need to let loose. Because if I did, those thoughts would catch an icy breeze and swirl through the air wild and free, leaving chaos in their wake. I didn't have time or room for that in my life.

Instead, I fixed my gaze on the passing storefronts with their holiday displays. Six-foot-tall toy soldiers stood on either side of the bookshop's entrance. Lucy's bakery had a queue of bundled-up customers that wrapped around the front of her shop to check out her gorgeous gingerbread house window display. Jamie must have noticed the switch in my mood because he stayed quiet.

By some Christmas miracle, Jamie found a parking space directly in front of the post office. Thank God because I had been willing to negotiate some borderline sketchy stuff to not have to carry these packages for fifteen minutes in the cold.

Once he parked, Jamie faced me. "Penny. I-uh…"

As he hesitated, I let myself look at him, really look at him in all the ways I never allowed myself to. I took in the way his chestnut hair was perpetually messy like he ruffled his fingers through it multiple times a day and how his long nose might have looked too long on someone else's face, but on him, it was the perfect size. His lips appeared soft even though I'd never seen him use ChapStick in the five years I'd known him and his five o'clock shadow sported hints of copper and black growth mixed in with the brown.

Warm air flowed from the vents and felt scorching all the sudden.

"I'm gonna get some air," I said as I felt for the door handle without breaking eye contact.

"Wait. What you said before…"

"It was nothing. I'm tired. Long day. You know how it is." I continued my assault of the door panel so frazzled that I thought the cup holder was my intended target.

"You can always count on me. Even after you…" He paused and tipped his head back on the headrest. "Even after you're married, we'll be friends. We'll always be friends."

My fingers finally found the handle. As I pulled it, opening the door, I forced a grin.

"Yup. Friends," I said. The crisp sobering air hit my face as I unfolded out of the car and faced the post office. Jamie followed, or I thought he did based on the sound of his door creaking open. I took in a deep lungful of air. *Friends.*

Jamie cleared his throat at my side, and I turned to him.

"I'm going to run in and see if they have a cart or something," he said. "Otherwise, this will be a nightmare."

"Okay."

While he went inside, I busied myself with pulling out boxes from the backseat and stacking them on the passenger seat for easier access. As I grabbed my second load, I noticed a plain silver gift bag tucked behind Jamie's seat. It had to be his since Mrs. McCormick's were all boxed and ready for mailing.

Was it a gift that he received or was going to give?

Was it for a woman?

I had no business wondering that. I was getting married in two days. Although... he was my friend and thinking about it, he's never talked to me about girlfriends before. Have I been so selfish with my Scooter issues and work drama that I haven't asked?

The sound of wheels rolling over cracks in the sidewalk jolted me so hard that I bonked my head on the doorframe. "Shit."

"You okay? Did you smack your head?" he asked, pulling the cart sideways, so it stayed put.

"Mhm. I'm okay." I rubbed the crown of my head. "Glad they had a cart!"

"Lemme see," he said low.

My brow raised. See what?

But before I could ask, he was behind me, moving my palm and bringing his face close to the top of my head. So close that I could smell the cinnamon mint he popped in his mouth earlier mixed with his spicy pine aftershave. Gently, he rubbed the area where a small egg was most likely forming.

"Looks okay," he murmured. "You'll probably have a bump though. You don't know how many times a week I do the same thing." His soft laugh drifted so close to my ear that I wanted to catch it somehow. Turn the sound into a music box that only I could hear.

He backed away and I sucked in a breath. "I bet. I don't know how you fit in such a small car."

"It's worth it for the gas mileage. Plus, I'm not a truck guy," he chuckled. "Small SUV, maybe but never a truck."

I nodded. There certainly was a stark difference between truck guys and other guys like Jamie. I was so used to Scooter and his truck that the thought of Jamie in a truck seemed absurd.

"Let's get this loaded. I warned Mr. Healy that we were deeply sorry for the number of packages we were about to bring in. I gave him a cookie from the welcome bags for his trouble."

"Jamie! I didn't know you grabbed a cookie. Genius level idea."

"A little sugar goes a long way," he said with a grin.

We tag teamed. He pulled everything out, and I stacked them neatly. There were only four people ahead of us in line, which was another Christmas miracle. Even so, by the time we finished up, we were both very much in need of a break.

"Want to grab a coffee?" Jamie asked.

Brew Haven was only a short walking distance from the post office. I hadn't been there in a few months with the chaos of wedding planning and the thought of stepping foot inside had me grinning.

"Hmm... let me think about it," I teased. "Of course I want coffee. Anytime, anywhere. Plus it's freezing out here."

Penny,

I wish I was with you to see you smile when you realize what gift number four is. All I need to say is business card, and you'll know. I'd even bet you're laughing right now while reading this. As you probably guessed, I present to you the very last copy in existence (rarer than the mint condition Mickey Mantle baseball card or even the Princess Diana Beanie Baby) the Lameson Hart business card.

When I came into the break room that day with a full stack of cards with a typo, I never expected you to crack up the way you did. After I let on that I had already included them in dozens of sales folders at a vendor event the previous day, I honestly thought you might fall out of your chair.

You'd been pretty down that week. It was close to the holidays, so maybe that had something to do with it. But all I could think was that I'd have hundreds of people think my name was Lameson if it would put a smile on your face. I'd introduce myself to the president of the United States as Lameson if only to hear you laugh.

So anytime you're feeling down, pull out this card and know I'd do anything to see you smile.

-Jamie

Chapter 5

DECEMBER 23RD

Just like every other shop in town, Brew Haven was packed with tourists. Who could blame them when there were drinks on the menu called Reindeer Roast and Mistletoe Mocha? I let the warmth of being inside the cozy cafe thaw my frozen fingers as Jamie and I stood close in line.

"So what'll it be, Burke? Eggnog Express Latte with extra brown sugar or a Nutcracker Nectar? Whatever that is." He laughed.

A couple deep in conversation nudged past me on their way toward the exit, knocking me sideways. Jamie grabbed onto my waist to steady me, and his palms were so large that they covered half my torso.

"Crap." I huffed, looking behind me at the man holding a hot drink. "I almost made that guy spill his drink."

I looked down toward my waist where Jamie's hands still held me. He glanced behind him at the couple on their way out the door and loosened a breath.

"You okay?" he asked for what felt like the tenth time that day. If he kept asking, I may not be able to keep saying that I was okay because the way his palm felt against my waist had me feeling things I shouldn't be feeling. I cleared my throat and he dropped his hands to his sides.

"Yeah. Glad, for that guy's sake, that you have lightning-fast reflexes. This is the second time today you've stopped me from falling. You sure you need caffeine?"

We moved closer to the counter, as the man in front of us stepped up to give his order. Jamie laughed and the mood lightened again.

"If I'm going to get through the party tonight, yes, lots of caffeine. I may go with the Reindeer Roast. Let's hope it doesn't taste like a reindeer smells."

"Mmm, reindeer essence." I laughed. "It's probably loaded with mountains of sugar and chocolate syrup. You'll be buzzing all night."

I watched his face break into a wide grin and his dimples made an appearance. He bent to my ear level. "The sugar is well earned," and turned back toward the line with a wink.

Once it was our turn in line, Jamie ordered himself a Reindeer Roast and I ordered a Mistletoe Mocha minus my usual brown sugar. "There's Jack," Jamie gestured. I followed his gaze toward the floor where a man, even taller than Jamie's six feet three inches, was crouching under a sink fussing with a pipe.

"Hey Jack," Jamie called to his brother, "you'll scare away your customers with that plumber's crack."

Jack stood up and adjusted his pants with a scowl. "Nah, but they'll sure as hell run off when they catch sight of your ugly mug." Jamie laughed. This had to be the way brothers showed their affection. I wouldn't know.

We moved over so we didn't hold up the line, while Jack put his wrench down and scrubbed a hand over his face. He blinked, then noticed me standing next to Jamie.

"Oh hey, Penny. I didn't see you there next to Stretch. How's it going?"

I shook my head and laughed. "Pretty good, thanks. Business is booming huh?" Small talk was never my strongest trait.

He blinked and took in the line like he was just noticing the crowd of people. "Guess so."

"Still got that sitter for tonight?" Jamie asked, then turned to me to add, "This big dummy hasn't done any Christmas shopping for his kids yet."

Jack sighed and cursed under his breath. "Yeah, I'm heading out of here soon."

For his sake, I hoped for a Christmas miracle that the stores wouldn't be madhouses. I couldn't imagine how tough Jack had it being a single dad, especially around the holidays. I was lucky I had my mom as long as I did. The barista called our names to let us know our drinks were ready and we said our goodbyes to Jack. He went right back to fixing the leaky pipe.

We brought our steaming hot cups to a little table in the corner somewhat away from the hustle and bustle of the other customers.

"This is my first themed drink of the season," I confessed.

"Not a fan of peppermint?" he asked before taking a sip.

I raised my brows. "It's not that." We were having a good time. Why did I feel the need to bring it down? "It's nothing."

He took his lid off and blew some of the steam away. I couldn't help my eyes drifting to his pursed lips.

"I know it's a hard time of year for you," he said, casting his eyes down. "Because of your mom."

"Yeah," my voice cracked. "I try. Every year gets easier. But sometimes I look all around me at everyone drinking eggnog, wearing Santa hats, and being cheerful about one silly day, and I feel like it's too much to smile and pretend. It kills me because she loved the holidays so much."

I took a sip of my still-steaming drink, willing the chocolate to break me out of this funk.

"What was her favorite thing about Christmas?" My chest squeezed at the sincerity in his voice. He genuinely wanted to know.

"That's a tough one." I smiled, conjuring images of my mom from so long ago into my mind. "Sometimes the year that she was sick, before she passed, is what sticks out the most. It's been a long time since I've thought about the good memories, you know?"

I'd told Jamie years ago that my mom died from cancer when I was seventeen, lymphoma that spread to her brain. We weren't even friends then. I can't remember how the topic came up, but what stands out in my mind is how he didn't give me the usual I'm-sorry routine before changing the subject. He kept his eyes locked on mine and asked me about her. I hadn't talked about her to anyone in years, not Scooter and not even my dad except for him using her name in passing. Jamie looked at me then the way he was looking at me from across the table now. Steam from his drink drifted across his face, making him look otherworldly somehow.

"She loved the food most, I think. Feeding people made her happy. We always baked a million cookies and delivered them to everyone in town. I think her heart was the fullest when she was bringing joy to others."

I sighed but held the image of my mother's smile in my thoughts for a moment longer. When I looked up, Jamie's gaze was fixed on me.

"I see that in you also," he said. "Wanting to make everyone happy."

"Yeah. I guess that's why I've stayed at The Ridge for way too long." I chuckled, trying to lighten the mood. He leaned back and tapped his thumb on the edge of the table. "What about you? What's your favorite thing about the holidays?"

He ran a hand through his messy hair while his gaze stayed fixed on my face.

"Are *you* happy, Penny?"

"Am I happy?" I repeated his question as a bubble of nervous laughter threatened to escape. His hazel eyes searched mine, making me feel like a spotlight was shining on all the bits I wanted to keep hidden in the shadows. "I-I'm," I stammered. "Yeah... why wouldn't I be?"

What an uncomfortable question. This wasn't us. When he didn't respond, I looked back up at him. That same intense expression lined his features. I stared right back at him like we were in some sort of battle of wills. We joked around and helped each other out at work. We quoted *The Office* to each other and compared our coworkers to the cast members. And yeah, occasionally, we talked about deeper topics. But to come right out and ask me if I was happy? How could he?

The paper coffee cup in front of me suddenly became the most interesting thing in the world. I studied the red and green lettering that spelled out the word *merry* in different fonts until my phone rang, and he looked away.

I yanked it from my coat pocket and answered without even seeing who was calling me.

"Hey, babe," Scooter said. "Can you hear me?"

"Hey. Where are you? It's super loud." I could barely hear him because of the background noise.

"Bachelor party. A few of the guys took me to happy hour to celebrate. Can you get a ride home?"

I closed my eyes and rubbed the spot on my temple where a headache was forming. Jamie raised his brows, clearly listening to my conversation.

"What about the party tonight?" I asked. He was supposed to come with me since he bailed on it last year. He promised.

"Oh man, babe. That's tonight? I forgot all about it," he yelled over the music in the background. "I'll make it up to you, okay?"

I wouldn't let Jamie see me upset. Not after the whole, are you happy question. I plastered on a smile.

"Okay. That's fine. Be safe," I said clipped and to the point, so that hopefully Jamie wouldn't pry.

I hung up, wanting nothing more than to be home in my pajamas.

"Everything okay?"

"Yeah." I flashed a grin even though it felt like I was pushing against weighted cheeks.

A muscle ticked in his jaw, but he stayed quiet. At least I could be grateful that he had dropped the happiness question. I drained my cup and let the mocha goodness radiate warmth throughout my belly.

"We should probably get going," I said. My chair scraped against the worn wooden floor as I pushed to stand. "Do you mind dropping me off at home? I have to get ready for the party and grab my Secret Santa gift."

"Sure."

We walked back to his car through the brisk early evening air. Christmas lights glowed and carols drifted onto the sidewalk from shop doors opening. I couldn't help but notice the shift in Jamie's mood. Picking up on minuscule changes in people's energy was kind of a superpower of mine. It's the one thing that's helped me avoid too much drama with Scooter and his family. I'd sense a mood shift and pivot. I was always watching for small changes in body language and tone. It was easier to be proactive and know when to keep quiet with Scooter, but I didn't remember the first time I realized I'd been doing the same thing with other people too.

I wasn't dumb enough to ignore the signs that Jamie wasn't Scooter's biggest fan. But at this point, I'd been with Scooter for too long to back out. He was there for me when grief had shackled itself to my bones and I couldn't move, let alone plan my life. Plus, he needed me. We'd made plans for the future. I would stay home and raise our children, and he'd be more caring once he's a husband and a father. I just knew it.

Whatever feelings I had toward Jamie were nothing more than friendship-based. Even if the looks he kept throwing me from the driver's side cracked my heart in two.

He pulled into the driveway of my small two-bedroom house. The one Scooter and I bought right out of high school with the life insurance money from my mother's policy. He loved the place because of its large two-car garage where he could store his off-road vehicles and make a man cave. I'd been so grief-stricken that I had agreed, and I had grown to love the place. Especially my tiny office space in the spare bedroom. It had an old, refurbished desk in front of a window overlooking the maple tree in the backyard. It's my favorite spot to sit and write. However, it'd become more of a storage space for wedding decor and overflow. The physical piles of stuff that came with planning a wedding had been the only thing Scooter's mother hadn't wanted to take over.

"Do you want me to pick you up for the party?" he asked. I tried to read his tone but couldn't figure him out. He hadn't spoken a word since the cafe and now he was offering me a ride.

"It's okay. I can drive myself." I rubbed at my throbbing temple before turning to face him. "Thanks again for helping me today... and for the bars... and the coffee a—"

He cupped my face with both hands, and before I had a second to register what was happening, he kissed me. Heat spread throughout my body as I grabbed his shoulders and brought myself closer to him. I didn't want to think about the shock rolling through my system. I only wanted to feel. And God, the way he moved his lips against mine was soft with an urgency I had never felt before. His palm fisted in my hair gently, and I melted even more.

His lips were so soft and warm. Softer than Scooter's.

Shit. Scooter.

I couldn't do this. Even though need coursed through me like an electric current. I was getting married in two days.

I pulled back, connecting with Jamie's heated gaze. We were both panting as unspoken thoughts swirled between us like a mountain that needed to be climbed.

"I'm sorry—" he started, as I said the same thing at the same time.

"I can't...I..." I couldn't think straight. Without another word, I grabbed my purse, yanked the door open, and jogged into my house as fast as I could.

Penny,

The next gift is different from the rest. I saw this pen at the bookstore and knew you had to have it. No self-deprecating jokes allowed, Burke. I know it says Future Bestselling Author on it, which is why I got it for you. I believe in you. Your writing is incredible, and the way you put thoughts to paper blows my mind.

It took you a while to share anything you've written with me, but when you did, I finally uncovered that hidden piece of you that had been missing. Your stories are a part of you. They're engrained so deep that to keep them hidden is to keep yourself hidden too.

I'll always be your number one fan, and anyone who gets a chance to read your work is incredibly lucky.

—Jamie

Chapter 6

DECEMBER 23RD

My pulse didn't calm down until I watched out my living room window as Jamie pulled away.

He just kissed me.

That really happened. And I kissed him back.

I felt like a hot iron had branded me a cheater with red letters across my forehead. Guilt gnawed my insides, but I couldn't tell Scooter what happened. He'd kill Jamie. And if I was being honest with myself, I needed to sort out my feelings. I'd never seen Jamie as more than my best friend. Yes, he was attractive, and my body noticed, but he'd never let on that he felt anything for me in that way.

I scrambled around my bedroom and flipped on another Christmas episode of *The Office* for background noise. The party was starting in an hour, and I had to be there. Gary would never let it go if I bailed. Plus, I needed to talk to Jamie about the kiss. And I didn't want to have that conversation over the phone.

But what would you even say? My nagging inner voice asked as I sifted through my closet for the black dress I wore for special occasions. I'd tell him it was a mistake. A moment of weakness between two close friends.

I traded my work button up and skirt for the curve-hugging black dress and took some time to de-frizz and tame my wild curls. After applying a bit of make-up, I stood back and looked at myself in my bathroom mirror. It had been months since I dressed up. I hardly recognized the woman staring back at me. Had the kiss with Jamie changed me that much?

Fifteen minutes later, I carried my Secret Santa gift for Paula out to my car. My skin pebbled in the cool air as I waited for what seemed like forever for my old Camry to warm up.

As I drove by houses lit with sparkling lights and dim shop windows closed for the evening, I willed myself to be strong. This was going to be another lame work party. I'd stay for an hour or two, eat something, then come home one day closer to being a married woman.

Except the moment I walked into the banquet hall, I knew this party was something different. Instrumental Christmas carols drifted through speakers in the corner of the room where at least two dozen of my fellow employees mingled around tables. Everyone was dressed far nicer than I'd ever seen, in festive reds and silvers. Divine smells from the kitchen area were already permeating the space, making my mouth water. My heels clicked against the marble floor as I made my way across the room. Emmy was deep in conversation with Mel, one of our friends from housekeeping when I joined them around a table.

"They really went all out," I said, admiring the sprigs of evergreen and golden-hued candles.

"It beats what Paula was originally going to use. Dollar-store snow-men figurine centerpieces," Emmy laughed. "Maybe someone important is coming tonight."

She waggled her brows and took a sip of white wine.

"Like who?" Mel asked. "They aren't letting any hotel guests in."

I pulled a chair out and took a seat. My feet were so not used to standing in heels like the ones I was wearing.

"A little birdie told me the owner might show up."

Emmy pulled the chair beside me out and sat.

I reached for the pitcher of water even though everything in my being wanted a glass of wine. My nerves needed it after earlier. I'd rather not drink than have to bug someone to give me a ride home later.

"Can't be," I said. "He hasn't ever come in the almost ten years I've worked at this place. He's like some phantom rich guy who has about seven assistants to do his bidding."

"I've been here five years and I agree," Mel added. "I don't even think Mr. Woods speaks with him much."

"It is probably why he still has his job as manager," Emmy said with a smirk. She wasn't wrong. If Gary had any amount of oversight, he'd likely be long gone. He wasn't terrible at managing. We did well enough. He just wasn't very efficient. In a different scenario, with less capable employees, he'd be in deep water without a life vest.

"I'm going to keep my eyes peeled," Emmy said. "I've heard he's gorgeous, loaded, and very much single. I'd love to pick his brain on what got him into tourism. Maybe try to get info on any open internships in the city." She winked and sipped her wine.

I scoffed. "Do you even know his name? Or how about what he looks like?"

Emmy was great, but she was twenty-one with confidence I couldn't muster on my best day. I envied that about her. Plus, she didn't let the work rumor mill drag her down.

Mel raised her glass toward me. "Penny's right. We know nothing about the guy."

"Looks like I'll have to go get my information straight from the horse's mouth. Paula was the one spreading the rumor." She stood up and adjusted her barely-there dress. "See you, ladies."

I watched her head off in the direction of the gift table toward a very frazzled looking Paula.

"If I had a booty like hers, I'd take my chances too." Mel laughed and lifted her glass for me to cheers. "I guess it's just us old maids here. Speaking of, Amelia and Cass were supposed to be here already." She pulled her phone out from the purse slung along the back of the chair. "Let me see where they're at."

I nodded, then gestured toward the gift table. "Be right back."

I was already drained. Hopefully, they'd bring out the food soon and I could eat and be on my way. I reached the gift table and handed Paula my Secret Santa gift.

"Penny, thanks." She thrusted a clipboard at me. "Can you check off your name here? I'm keeping track of who has dropped off their gift. Don't want anyone to miss out."

"Sure." I scanned the list of over fifty employees' names. It seemed they were grouped by department instead of alphabetical order. My gaze passed by the sales staff and next to Jamie's name were his initials. I found my name on the second page and initialed with the attached pen. "Here you go, Paula."

She took the clipboard back and forced a smile. "Thanks, love. I'm sure you understand the stress of planning a big party like this especially with your wedding so soon and all."

I blinked slowly and nodded. "Yeah, it's hard work. For what it's worth, you've done an amazing job. The place looks magical."

She beamed and raised her chin. "Thanks. I had a little help. Some women who work for the owner came by this afternoon and helped me with the finishing touches. All the way from the city. They said Mr. Connor was going to show up tonight, and he liked everything perfect."

Emmy hadn't been exaggerating. Paula turned back to the gift table to organize wrapped packages and bags.

"I'm sure he'll be more than impressed." I smiled while glancing back at the clipboard in her hand. "Hey, Paula, have you seen Jamie?"

She turned and gave me a knowing look. "Poor guy. He wasn't feeling well. But he was sweet enough to drop off his Secret Santa gift before he went home to rest."

My shoulders sank. It was my fault. I'd probably ruined his Christmas by confusing him and messing up our friendship. I'd really hoped he would have been here to talk.

Paula must have seen the disappointment on my face because she squeezed my shoulder and flashed me a pitying smile. I left her to her task, waving to coworkers as I made my way back to the table.

Should I text him? I didn't want things to be even more awkward between us and who knows if I'd have time in the next few days. I glanced around the room at everyone conversing, drinking, and laughing. It didn't feel right without him here. I pulled my phone out of my bag and swiped until I got to his name.

Me: *Hey... miss you here.*

No, I couldn't say that. Not after what happened.
Delete.

Me: *Hey... are you feeling all right? Paula said you left sick.*

I tapped my heels to the beat of Jingle Bells as I waited. I couldn't blame him if he ignored my message. Guilt clawed at my insides. While I had my phone out, I figured I'd check in with Scooter too.

Me: *How's your night going?*

It must've been going better than mine. I spotted Gary across the room taking pictures with an expensive camera. He was wearing one of those crazy light up ties that had him standing out like a sore thumb. I smiled as I watched him bug some of the back-office staff to pose for a photo.

My phone beeped, and my pulse kicked up.

Scooter: *Thumbs up*

Sighing, I shoved my phone back into my bag as the kitchen staff started loading the buffet.

After eating and listening to the ladies from housekeeping gossip about a few of our regulars, I was more than ready to go home, but Gary had other plans. Somehow, he'd set up a microphone in front of the gift table and was tapping on it for attention. He'd changed into an over-the-top Santa suit, white beard and all.

"Ho-ho-hello, everyone! I've come down from the North Pole to bring you fine employees of The Ridge some holiday cheer." His voice boomed through the mic loud enough that the entire town could probably hear him. "Some of you have been very nice this year and some of you have been very naughty... I'm looking at you bell staff," he said while pointing their way.

"Will he get on with it?" a young woman from housekeeping grumbled under her breath. "My sitter just texted that she needs to leave soon."

I gave her a sympathetic smile. Gary loved to entertain a crowd... awkwardly. Jamie and I had this shared look we'd give each other anytime we were held hostage by a Gary Woods led meeting. If he were here, we'd have rolled our eyes at least five times.

"Who's ready for Secret Santa?" Gary asked like he was the new host of a Christmas themed game show. I clapped lightly, and the rest of the group gave a similar lukewarm response.

We weren't being ungrateful—maybe some people were—but it had been one of the busiest weeks of the year, and we were all bone tired. Every department had been working overtime and beyond their job requirements. They all surely felt like I did, which was ready to go home after a delicious meal.

Gary started calling out his version of nicknames from Paula's clipboard. They included classics like calling Mel, Melaroni and Cheese, or calling Chris, Chris Cross. He hollered Penjamin Button, which was one of my more ridiculous nicknames, and I looked up to find him gesturing to me.

Okay, I guess he wanted me to go up to the table... in front of everyone. This was fine. I pulled a breath in through my nose and stood up on my wobbly heels, hoping everyone was too deep in conversation to watch me.

Every step felt like a mile as my heels clinked against the marble. Gary clapped when I reached him as if I'd won an award.

"Penjamin, Merry Christmas," he said and handed me a gift bag. My eyes widened as soon as I saw it. The shiny silver bag that was in Jamie's car. Why hadn't he mentioned he was my Secret Santa earlier?

Gary was already calling another person up to get their gift as I made my way back to the table. But before I could get there, I heard a familiar voice calling my name from across the room.

Scooter?

What was he doing here?

He stumbled my way with two of his buddies from maintenance flanking him. They were clearly making sure he stayed upright. The night was about to suck even more.

"Pen," he slurred. "Babe. The guys wanted to come get their presents." That made sense. "Plus, they were tapped out, and they said it's open bar here."

His loud voice echoed off the high ceilings. I needed to get him home before he hit that open bar too hard. Glaring at his friends, I slung Scooter's arm around my shoulder.

"Come on. Tell me about your night." If I could get him talking and distracted, we could slip out of here.

"Everyone was buying me drinks. Why'd we wait so long to do this wedding thing, babe? It's like being king for a day."

"Uh huh," I nodded while pulling him toward the door and silently fuming. "I bet you loved that."

"Hell yeah. Best feeling I've had in a long time." He palmed my shoulder, then tried to reach lower for my breast. I swatted him away. All that attention must have gotten him in the mood.

"Not here, Scooter. We're at work."

He pouted in my ear. "Let's get a room, babe. I'm feeling really good."

I wanted to say, you're probably feeling very little with the number of drinks you've had, but I kept quiet. I hoped he'd pass out as soon as we got home.

✿ • ❋ ❆ ❋ • ✿

Somehow, I managed to get him into my car and home in one piece. Holding up most of his weight, I led him toward the bedroom after having dropped my gift from Jamie and purse in the entryway.

"You look hot tonight, babe," he said as I led him to his side of the bed. He reached out, drifting his palm across my shoulder again. "How come you don't dress like this all the time?"

His eyes darkened with his silent request.

Two more nights until I was to be a married woman. May as well get used to nights like these.

Penny,

The first summer I started at the hotel, a group of us were walking over to Brew Haven for coffee after our shifts. I was pretty shy and awkward with you at that point. I cringe now at how very Lameson I was. I hope you never noticed.

The sun cast shades of gold over everything that evening. It was like outside the hotel was another world, with its lush trees bathed in light, and you were an ethereal goddess. Your skin glowed. Your hair curled from the heat and swung loose at your back. I couldn't even tell you who else went with us on that walk. They were extras, and you were the star. I couldn't keep my eyes off you even though I tried. That was the week I found out you were engaged. I'd be lying if I said it didn't crush me. Halfway there, you stopped, crouched on the sidewalk, and plucked a dandelion from a crack in the concrete.

I noticed how you rubbed the tip of your finger against its sunny yellow petals and then laughed at something someone said.

I took a deep breath and worked up the nerve to talk to you. I asked why you picked that dandelion. You told me that, "even though something is considered a weed doesn't mean it isn't beautiful." We went on our way, but that stayed with me all these years.

Now every time I pass a dandelion on a walk, I think of you. I pressed this one between glass so you'll always remember that day and your words of wisdom.

—Jamie

Chapter 7

DECEMBER 24TH

Since Scooter and I have been together, we've always spent Christmas Eve at his parents' house. This year was no exception. Barbara flitted around with a glass of wine in one hand and her cellphone in the other taking pictures for her social media of her picture-perfect holiday. Scooter Sr. was three whiskeys in and watching sports in the finished basement with my extremely hungover fiancé. One of Scooter's cousins and her husband chatted with a few of the aunts and uncles in the formal living room while their kids ran circles around the house. We were still waiting on Russell and Trisha as well as a neighbor who usually joined us on holidays.

I did my best to hide out in the family room of their huge colonial as I got my quality time in with Scooter's childhood dog, Roofus, who was also hiding from the beast children. He made himself scarce after they tried to wrap him with Christmas bows last year.

"Roofussss," eight-year-old Jimmy called. I scratched the old guy's scruffy ears.

"Don't worry, Roofus, I think we're safe in here."

I was having a conversation with a dog. I was losing my mind, but he was much better company than the family in the other rooms.

We'd be opening gifts soon. Together. In front of the tree where Barbara would give a running commentary on what each person opened. Maybe I could hide with the dog the whole day.

Wishful thinking.

My phone sat on the coffee table in front of me, pulling at my attention like a beacon. Jamie never responded to my message. I kept telling myself he was busy; it was Christmas, and he usually spent it at his parents' house in Connecticut with Jack and the kids. He'd already RSVP'd no to the wedding weeks ago for that reason. An ache spread throughout my chest when I thought about losing him. He was my best friend, the person I went to when I had something funny happen to me or needed to get something off my chest. He was my person.

"Penny, it's time for gifts. Everyone's here." Barbara's voice cut through my thoughts, and I groaned. I gave Roofus one more scratch before facing the worst part of the day.

"Cootie, love, hold it up so everyone can see it," Barbara crooned.

"Christ, Mom. I've told you not to call me that," Scooter said, which pulled a sharp hiss from his ultra-religious Grandma. If he noticed, he didn't acknowledge her instead he held up a blue and pink Hawaiian shirt, something he'd never wear, for all to see. "Thanks, Mom, it's great."

"You'll look so handsome in it on your trip." She was talking about our honeymoon to Hawaii next week. Knowing Scooter, he'd only wear that if he were at least three drinks deep. Trisha was the only other member of the family with any sense at all, and she glanced my way and smirked. She wasn't immune to the travesty that was a Barbara Anderson gift.

"Barb, let the boy open his gift from me now," Scooter Sr. called. It was the first sentence I'd heard him utter all day.

Barbara shuffled gifts around the beautifully decorated tree, careful not to spill her wine. She found a small, unwrapped box adorned with a simple red ribbon.

"Dad?" Scooter asked with his brow cocked. His father gestured for him to open it. I knew it was something significant since Barb put her wine down and got her phone camera ready.

Scooter's entire face lit up in the first smile I'd seen from him all day. Everyone else started whooping and saying things like "it's about time". I was confused but Scooter wasn't.

"What is it?" one of the young cousins said while she played with her new doll's hair.

"It's the family legacy, dear," Barbara said. "Your great-uncle Scooter's grandfather bought that Rolex almost a hundred years ago."

"I can't believe that thing's still kicking," Russell said. "Congrats, man."

Scooter got up from his seat next to the tree and went to shake his father's hand. Then his mother came around to hug him from behind. Watching this was like being an outsider looking in.

"Now that you're finally getting married, I knew it was time," Scooter Sr. said. "One day, you can pass it down to your son."

My stomach churned, then Scooter turned and met my gaze with a proud look.

"Come look, babe. I don't know if you remember me telling you about the watch but look. Isn't it amazing?"

I crossed the room, trying to drown out the chatter from the others while the kids ripped open another gift, and I peered at it. It was a nice watch, solid and well built. I glanced at Barbara who had tears in her eyes from the whole exchange, and I smiled.

"It's great, congratulations," I said. He kissed my cheek and pulled me back to the couch beside him while he traced the links on the band with a gentle touch.

"Don't think we forgot about you, Penny," Barbara said. "I have the perfect gift for the new bride."

I held my breath and hoped it'd be something sweet like the watch. Obviously not a family heirloom, of course because I was lucky to have my engagement ring as it was. But maybe something I could wear tomorrow? She rustled around behind the tree making so much noise moving packages that everyone went quiet again waiting to see what she was doing.

Scooter squeezed my thigh with a huge grin on his face. "Do you know?" I whispered.

He shook his head. "No, but it must be good. She's been excited about it for a week."

I turned back toward the tree to see Barbara holding a box that was about half her height.

"It was stuck back there," she said. "Penny, Merry Christmas from Scooter Sr. and me." She brought the box directly in front of me and took two steps back.

"Thank you, wow. This is big, isn't it?" Thoroughly intrigued, I tore off the first sheet of wrapping paper, which exposed the front of the box. My jaw clenched as soon as I saw what it was.

Seriously?

She bought me a vacuum. A freaking vacuum for Christmas.

They were all watching me and waiting for my response. Each person grinned expectantly except for Trisha who looked like she was going to cry with me. I wish I knew if Barbara actually thought this was a good gift for her soon-to-be daughter-in-law. Was she trying to imply, once again, that I don't keep a tidy home because that's complete bull.

"Isn't it great? It's the latest model! I got it for a steal. You'll need that once the little ones start making messes."

Little ones? She was acting like I was already pregnant. I glanced at Scooter, still beaming at his watch entirely unfazed. All I could do to not either break down and cry or lose it was to stuff it down. I pushed the feeling down to mix with the concoction of confusion that was already brewing in my gut. I smiled and nodded.

"Thank you," I said through gritted teeth. "So much."

"Yeah, Mom, that's great. Pen really needs to clean more," Scooter laughed. "You nailed it."

The room broke out in laughter. Russell actually slapped his freaking knee, which garnered a smack on the arm from his wife. Heat crept up my face, and I yanked Scooter's hand from my thigh and pushed up from the couch. What was wrong with these people? I bolted from the room as Scooter called after me. Air. I had to get air.

I felt like an idiot. It'd been years of this. Why would I have thought this year would be any different? That I'd be treated like family? My fiancé didn't see a problem with the gift even though I'd told him year after year that his mother's gifts were demeaning. He always said I was overreacting because that's just how she was. Even when I bought her the nicest bath products, organic and handmade, or cashmere sweaters far out of my price range. It didn't matter. To her, I was nothing more than a vessel who would bear her grandchildren sooner rather than later.

I grabbed my phone and pushed through the front door. Brisk air hit my face, and I rubbed my eyes, realizing I'd been crying. My nose ran, and I cursed myself for not grabbing my coat.

"I'm so stupid," I said to myself.

Each exhale clouded my vision while I paced the length of their front porch. Rubbing my hands together for warmth, I let a few more minutes pass while I gathered my thoughts. Scooter hadn't come out to find me. No surprise there. He was probably already back downstairs with a drink in his hand, watching TV.

When I started to shake from the cold, I went back inside. Trisha was sitting on a leather bench inside the entryway. I jumped, not expecting to see someone right there. I had to get out of that house and clear my head.

"Trisha, oh my God, you scared me."

"Sorry. I peeked outside and saw you pacing. I figured I'd give you some alone time."

She patted the seat next to her, and I joined her. I couldn't get my legs to stop trembling from a mixture of cold and the surge of emotions. I let my gaze fall on the painting ahead of me instead of facing her sympathetic look. Trisha patted my shoulder. I sighed.

"Why do we stay?" It was almost like she was asking herself rather than me.

I let out a cynical laugh. "When you figure that out, let me know."

"For what it's worth, I don't know if I would have made it this long without you in the family," she said.

I turned to meet her eyes. "Same."

Shuffling sounds and loud conversation had us shifting our gazes toward the living room. The gift exchange must have been ending.

"If you want to go, I can cover for you. It's your freaking wedding day tomorrow," she sighed. "You shouldn't spend today crying over Bitchy Barbara."

I laughed. "Bitchy Barbara has a nice ring to it." If only she knew that my emotions were for more reasons than my insensitive soon-to-be moth-er-in-law. "It's almost dinner. I may as well stay and not rock the boat."

Trish grinned and slung an arm around my shoulder. "I'm glad for entirely selfish reasons. I really didn't want to be stuck alone, as much as I'd understand you wanting to leave. Let's go have a drink. Last time we were here, Russ showed me where Barb keeps the good stuff."

I let her lead me back into the commotion but tiny pieces of my heart chipped away with each step we took from the front door.

Hours later, I finally gathered my things to head home. As soon as the first guest announced they were finished eating, I figured it was acceptable for me to excuse myself also. Scooter was slurring his words, and Russell wasn't far behind him. We'd already planned for them to sleep at Scooter's parent's house, so there was no need for me to stay and witness his inebriation.

He followed me to the door where I held nothing but my purse, insisting I'd have Scooter bring my special Christmas present home later that week.

"Pen." Scooter took my palm in his hand and squeezed gently. I felt a drunken speech coming on, one that I'd normally cut off and redirect, but with the taste of Jamie's kiss still lingering and my guilt about it sitting low in my gut, I let him go on. "You gon be my wife tomorrow. Affer allll this fucking time, I still want you. I still need you to take care of me for always." His eyes bore into mine, glazed over but tender, and I hung my head to avoid making eye contact. "'M sooo lucky, babe. You're gon be the best mom. Just like mine mom." *What?* "And I know you're gon be there for me no matter what."

He tipped my chin up and kissed me. His breath tasted of whiskey and onion gravy from dinner. When he opened his mouth to slip his tongue into mine, I pulled back. He didn't seem to notice my lack of reciprocation.

"Bye, Scoot," I said and pulled the front door open. "I'll see you tomorrow, okay? Don't let Russell get you too drunk."

He chuckled, then wiped moisture off his lips. "Oh, he's gon give it to me good. My last night as a free man."

I shook my head and stepped out into the frigid evening air. Scooter shut the door, but not before I took one more look at him to take in every detail of the man I was about to marry.

Waiting for my car to warm up in the driveway, I sat with those details. When I looked at Scooter, I didn't see him physically, not anymore, at least. I'd grown so used to his handsome features that, even with his lack of graceful aging, I still found things to find attractive. But it wasn't his looks that I saw tonight. It was the way he spoke to me. It was each sentence that started with *I* even in his drunken pre-wedding proclamation of love; he hadn't mentioned one thing he loved about *me*. Unless I counted the fact that he said I'd be a good mother... like his mother. If that was what his expectations were, he was living on another planet.

I stared at my reflection in the rearview mirror wondering who the woman looking back at me had become. My green eyes filled with tears and I knew, whoever she was, she wasn't me, not the real me. The real me was stuffed away ten years back and covered in a blanket of grief and complacency.

Only one person truly saw the real me, and it was time I figured out what to do.

Penny,

I know Christmas is hard for you. Losing your mom is a pain you'll carry for the rest of your life. When you've told me stories about her, I saw the mixture of joy and grief painted on your face, and I'd do anything to take that pain away.

Since I can't do that, I wanted to remind you of a good memory that you told me about, a piece of Christmas joy you can hold on to when the pain gets too deep.

My last gift to you is a Snoopy Christmas ornament. I know how much you loved to watch A Charlie Brown Christmas with her every year while you were growing up, laughing at Snoopy licking Lucy's face and imitating the dances they did together. I can picture you and your mom begging your dad to bring home a Charlie Brown tree every year when he prided himself on getting a big, full tree. Even then, you exuded love and care. I never got to know your mom, but I'm sure you learned that from her. She'd love the woman you've become and would want you to be happy and loved.

So, Burke, hang this Snoopy and know that she's with you this Christmas and always.

–Jamie

Chapter 8

DECEMBER 24TH

My home was too quiet and still. I needed a distraction, something to keep me focused and help me calm my racing thoughts. After locking up and turning on the living room light, I switched on a random episode of *The Office* for background noise. I changed into warm pajamas and sat on the couch, feeling on edge and restless.

On the drive home, I went over Scooter's words on a loop, with each cycle anger swelled inside me. I needed Jamie. He always knew the exact right things to say to help me feel better. But he was avoiding me and stewing on that thought dug a knife deeper into my fragmented heart.

I had to try again. Whatever issues I had going on with Scooter or his family didn't matter. Jamie was my friend, my best friend, and we needed to talk about what happened.

Pulling a deep breath in through my nose, I scrolled to his name in my contacts and hit call. My hand twitched as I held the phone in front of me, and I itched to toss it aside and run to the bathroom to vomit.

He didn't want to talk to me. I'd hurt him.

On the fourth ring, his gravelly voice came through the speaker. I closed my eyes and leaned my head back against the couch cushion.

"Burke? Is everything okay?"

We rarely, if ever, called each other on the phone. Texting was our thing when we weren't together or at work. Of course he was worried. I should have texted him first to see if he could talk. I swallowed the lump in my throat.

"Hey, yeah, I'm fine."

I'm really not. Why was it so hard to say what I wanted to say?

He stayed quiet for a moment, and our breathing was the only sound between us. I knew he was waiting for me to talk; he did that a lot. Most people had to fill the awkward silences but not Jamie.

"Okay. Maybe I'm not fine. We need to talk about the kiss, Jamie." I stood up and paced around my living room.

"I'm sorry," was all he said. He was waiting for me to say more. Waiting for me to say that I wasn't sorry. Not really. Yes, I felt like crap for cheating on Scooter, but I had needed that kiss to open my eyes and my heart to the man standing in front of me and to re-awaken something inside myself that I hadn't realize had died along with my mother all those years ago.

"Are you really sorry?" I exhaled. "Because I keep telling myself I should be, but I'm not. I..." I took a breath in front of the unlit Christmas tree and let the words dancing on the tip of my tongue rest before releasing them. "I'm not sorry, Jamie. Tell me right now that it was a mistake, and I'll forget it ever happened. But I don't want to lose you."

"Penny...," he breathed. I could picture my name falling from his soft lips as he sat alone in the dark wherever he was.

"I can't lose you," I cried.

"Did you look in the bag?"

I looked toward the entryway and saw it still sitting there. The silver gift bag from my best friend. How could I have forgotten about it?

"Not yet. I didn't have time," I stuttered. "Scooter was—"

"Open the bag, Penny. Open it tonight." His voice held an intensity I'd never heard from him before. I rolled my lip between my teeth in both worry and desire.

"What is it?" I didn't know if I had the strength to look without some forewarning of what I'd find.

"Open the bag and you'll see."

I stood on shaky legs and retrieved the bag. It felt heavier than I remembered. Maybe it was just heavy because I had been carrying a much heavier Scooter inside at the same time.

Bringing my phone to my ear, I murmured Jamie's name, but he didn't answer. He'd hung up. Curiosity replaced panic and suddenly I needed to know what was inside this bag more than I needed air to breathe. Layers of red tissue paper concealed whatever was in there, beckoning me to reach in and peek beneath them.

I sat back on the couch and placed the bag in front of me. Dwight's voice stopped as I hit pause on my show. I needed to give whatever was in there my full focus.

Reaching in, I pulled out the top layer of tissue and tossed it to the side. My hand landed on a book, so I took that out first. A few other small items were underneath the book, so I pulled them out as well and laid each thing along my table.

I grinned, recognizing some of the items like a name tag, a business card, and a brown sugar packet, but a few of the other things needed more explanation. My gaze focused on the black spiral-bound notebook with its hard canvas cover. I opened it and read each line reverently as if every page were a precious artifact.

Tears slid down my cheeks and my hands trembled. I touched every item that he'd so lovingly gathered and read the notes he'd written about them. The stories swirled through my mind each playing like a film. When

I reached the entry about my mom, my heart clenched, but knowing that he remembered those small details about my childhood filled me with emotion.

Then I reached the last page.

Fear had me locked in its grip. What if I was losing him for good? I forced myself to read each word, slowly taking them in.

PENNY,

YOU'VE REACHED THE END OF YOUR GIFTS. I HOPE THEY'VE BROUGHT A SMILE TO YOUR BEAUTIFUL FACE.

MAYBE I'M TAKING THE EASY PATH IN WRITING THESE NOTES, I DON'T KNOW. BUT, AS JIM SAYS, "CHRISTMAS IS THE TIME TO TELL PEOPLE HOW YOU FEEL," AND I COULDN'T GO ANOTHER CHRISTMAS, LET ALONE ANOTHER DAY, WITHOUT YOU KNOWING THAT I'M IN LOVE WITH YOU. YOUR MIND, YOUR HEART, YOUR SOUL.

I'M SO FUCKING IN LOVE WITH YOU, BURKE, THAT I'D RATHER DIE THAN SEE YOU UNHAPPY.

DON'T MARRY HIM. PLEASE DON'T DO IT. EVEN IF YOU DON'T RECIPROCATE MY FEELINGS, YOU DESERVE SO MUCH MORE.

YOU DESERVE TO BE THE CENTER OF SOMEONE'S WORLD, TO BE RESPECTED, FOR YOUR THOUGHTS AND FEELINGS TO BE LISTENED TO AND CHERISHED, AND TO BE DESIRED SO BADLY THAT THEY PHYSICALLY ACHE WHEN THEY'RE NOT TOUCHING YOUR SOFT SKIN.

YOU DESERVE A BEST FRIEND AND SOULMATE.

LOVE,

JAMIE

Oh my God.

He's in love with me. My best friend, my Jamie, loved me. How had I not seen it? Or maybe I had seen it but wouldn't let myself consider the truth.

I flipped back to the beginning and read the whole thing again and again, letting his words wash over me and absorb into my being.

Closing the book, I held it to my chest and paced the floors. Every one of Jamie's words struck true in my heart. I deserved happiness and love. Scooter had been that person at one time, but playing back our memories, I couldn't think of a single moment in the past five years that he'd shown me an ounce of what I deserved.

I'd spent so long believing he'd change and that I'd be selfish and disloyal to ask for what I needed. I was a fool. Jamie had told me what I'd desperately needed to hear and what no one else in my life had been strong enough to tell me. Scooter wasn't the one, and I deserved more.

My phone sat powered off on the table. I wanted to text Jamie. He was probably freaking out knowing I'd read every thought in his heart and mind. *Crap*. What would I say? I had to get my thoughts straight and then talk to Scooter. Whether Scooter deserved that or not, I needed the conversation.

The chances were that he'd be passed out drunk, but I couldn't waste any more time. I knew what I deserved, and I wanted to spend every second I could chasing that happiness.

I'd make Scooter listen to me.

Chapter 9

DECEMBER 24TH

By the time I bundled up and drove over to the Anderson's, it was nearing ten o'clock. A light snow fell from the sky and covered the walkway in powder. I breathed in the fresh smell in the air mixed with pine from the wreath hung on their front door, willing myself to be strong no matter what happened inside.

I rang the bell. While I waited, I bit my bottom lip with nervous energy. Flakes landed on my coat and melted into damp spots. After a few breaths, I rang the bell again even though every fiber of my being screamed at me to leave. I was being a bother.

Moments later, the door creaked open to reveal Barbara in her pale pink robe, slippers, and eye mask pulled above her forehead.

"Penny, what in the world are you doing out here?"

She rubbed her arms from the assault of brisk air and gestured me inside.

"I need to speak to Scooter. Is he awake?" I searched the darkened entryway for signs of guests, but all seemed quiet. Barbara shifted onto one foot and retied her robe string.

"What is this about?" She evaded my question. "He needs his rest for the wedding, and so do you. You should get home before you wake the whole house."

I went to take a step forward, but she blocked my path.

"Barb, this is important. I wouldn't be here if it wasn't." I said, my patience with this woman was wearing thin. As much as I wanted to tell her off for all the years that she'd treated me horribly, it was her son that needed to hear it. He should have been the one to stand up to her, not me, but if she didn't butt out and let me find Scooter, I'd give her a piece of my mind.

She sighed and straightened her posture. "What is it? You can tell me, and I'll take care of it. Scooter never has to know." Her eyes narrowed, looking me up and down. "Did you do something to my Cootie?"

Was she serious?

"No. God, you are delusional." I worried my bottom lip between my teeth. "Listen, Barb, this is between Scooter and me, okay? I'll go find him."

She blocked my way again, this time putting a palm out in front of me.

"You're not going through with it, are you?" she asked, voice low. "It's over?"

I met her gaze, searching her cold blue eyes for any signs of love or compassion. I only found resignation.

"Yes. It's over. And—"

I began to explain myself even though she didn't deserve an explanation.

"He's not here." She hung her head low. "He left earlier with Russell. I don't know where they went. I warned him if he was late tomorrow, I'd cut him out of my will."

Great, they probably went back out to the bars, which meant they definitely weren't in Greyridge. There was nothing open in town on Christmas Eve, not even the diner.

"I'll call him," I said, pulling out my phone.

Barbara reached out and held my wrist. "Don't bother. Whatever he's doing, he won't be in a state to hear what you have to say." She was right, as much as I didn't want to admit it. "Go home, Penny. I'll tell Scooter in the morning."

I stood inches from the front door thinking over her offer. What she wanted would be the easy way out. She'd soften the blow and deal with the aftermath, but I couldn't talk to Jamie without first talking to Scooter.

"Okay. You're right." Her shoulders caved in relief. I'd tell her what she wanted to hear and then go do what I needed to do.

"You would have been a great mother to my grandchildren," she said with quiet acceptance. "Merry Christmas."

"You too."

I stepped away from her and let myself out feeling lighter than I'd felt in a long time. Sitting in my car in the driveway, I let myself look at the Anderson's house and consider how glad I was that I'd never have to step foot inside there again. There was someone I could call to find Scooter, and I hated to bother her.

Trisha's phone rang and rang, and my chest clenched. Finally, before her voicemail would have come on, she answered with a groggy hello.

"Hey, Trish, I'm sorry to wake you."

"What's wrong? Is Russ okay?" she asked with alarm in her voice.

"Yes, or at least I think so. Let me start over. I need to find Scooter. Do you know where they went?"

I let the warm air thaw my frozen fingers while waiting for her to respond. She didn't answer right away, so I asked again in case she fell asleep.

"I'm not sure about the address... but they have a place they go sometimes over in Scranton. I was hoping you'd never find out about it," she whispered.

My mind whirled wondering what she could possibly be talking about.

"What are you saying?"

"It's a..." She hesitated. I wished I could reach through the phone and shake her. "Lifestyle club."

"I still don't know what you're saying?" I asked.

"It's a sex club. I'm sorry, Pen. I should have told you when I found out."

A sex club? Did I hear her right? My jaw dropped open as I tried to comprehend what that even meant.

"I-I don't even know what to say," I stammered. "You knew about this?"

"I found out a couple of months ago." I heard the unmistakable sound of her lighting a cigarette. "Russ and I have a different type of marriage. It's not physical if you know what I mean."

"You let your husband go to a sex club and sleep with other people?" I asked. I wasn't here to judge their marriage, to each their own as long as it's legal and no one was getting hurt.

"He does what he wants as long as he uses protection. I don't need to know the rest. It's unconventional, but it works for us."

"I'm not here to judge, Trish. I just need to find Scooter, but what you're saying is that my fiancé is off sleeping with someone else the night before our wedding?"

The realization hit me like a ton of bricks. All those nights he came home exhausted saying he had been at Hooters with Russell and the guys. He could have been at that club? Who else knew about this?

"I don't know," she exhaled. "I was going to tell you, but I didn't think it was my place. I'm sorry, Penny."

I bit down on my lip again to hold in what I wanted to say. She was supposed to be my friend. What was that conversation earlier? I took a deep breath and asked her for the name of the place before I hung up. My anger didn't need to be directed toward Barbara or Trisha. It was Scooter who deserved every bit of my suppressed rage.

Twenty-five minutes later, I pulled up to The Dream, Scranton's only private lifestyle club. From the outside the building looked similar to a small hotel, albeit a very private one with blacked-out windows. Snow was still falling in powdery flakes, covering the cars in the dimly lit lot. It didn't take much searching to find Russell's truck among the others thanks to his oversized blue bumper sticker that read, "If you think my tires are big you should see my dipstick." Scooter doubled over laughing the day Russell showed it to him while I rolled my eyes.

I had no idea what I'd be walking in to. Would there be people having sex all over the place like a giant orgy? Would I find Scooter like that? As much as things were over between us, I didn't think I could handle seeing him like that. I had to be strong though. This was the first step to reclaiming my happiness.

The front door opened into a small hallway where a large bouncer sat on a stool. He looked me over. His brow raised, and he asked for my ID and membership card.

"I'm not a m-member," I stuttered. His eyes bore into mine, and I straightened my posture. "I'm here to talk to someone."

"Sorry, lady. No membership, no entry."

Crap. I had to get in there.

"Well, what do I need to do to become a member?" I asked. He looked me over from head to toe. With what I was wearing, I looked like I was headed to a knitting circle not a sex club.

"Listen," he sighed. "There's been a recent change in ownership. You didn't hear that from me. All I know is, the membership structure is gonna be changing after the new year."

I nodded along, pretending I cared what he was talking about.

"Being that it's Christmas, I'll do you this good deed." He stood up, opened the door, and stepped aside to let me pass. "But you never saw me."

"Thanks." I placed a hand on his meaty forearm to show my gratitude but thought better of it when he darted his tongue out to lick his bottom lip.

The door opened to a room that looked no different from an upscale bar. It could have been any bar in America with its dim lighting, black walls, and dark floors. Light bounced off top shelf liquor bottles casting a sheen on the red leather stools that were pushed in against ebony wood. About a dozen people sat perched on them while others stood around mingling and talking. I couldn't hear much over the steady beat of house music playing, but I noticed a few women dressed in Santa and Mrs. Claus lingerie.

I didn't see Scooter or Russell among them, and my heart sank even more. If they weren't here, that meant they were probably somewhere more private.

"Hello there," an older man donning a red silk Santa robe greeted me. "You look lost."

I cleared my throat. "Um, I'm looking for someone actually... my fiancé."

He chuckled. "Uh oh, Santa's in trouble with Mrs. Claus I see."

I tapped my foot impatiently, wanting to get out of this place as quickly as I could.

"Can you help me? His name is Scooter. He's about six feet tall, brown hair. He's probably drunk and with his cousin, Russell."

The man chuckled again and heat rose to my cheeks. I forced a breath in through my nose and got a lungful of his strong cologne.

"It's against club rules to give out member information." He scratched his greying stubble. "But I could be persuaded..."

What the hell was wrong with this guy? As I was about to tell him to go to hell, a gorgeous woman in bright red lace lingerie that matched her hair interrupted us.

"Is he bothering you?" she asked before turning to him with a hand on her hip. "What did I tell you earlier? Three strikes and you're out, remember?"

He nodded, narrowing his gaze at her.

"Now scram. Go find someone who wants your attention, or I'll officially give you strike three."

He shuffled toward the bar, holding the large gap in his robe closed with a free hand. She turned back toward me and sighed.

"Sorry about him. The holidays get everyone extra sad and needy. He's harmless, just a bit creepy. Can I help you?"

She focused her dark eyes on me and took in my attire like the bouncer did. I flushed with embarrassment.

"Yes, I'm looking for my fiancé." I described Scooter again, and before I even had time to say his name, she stopped me.

"Scooter, right? Can't forget a name like that. He's here, drunk as hell. Bouncer almost threw him and his friend out until one of our regulars grabbed him and took him to a private room."

She must have noticed my face fall since she rubbed my shoulder softly.

"Come on, I'll lead you to him. But our secret, okay? I'm not supposed to do this. Just promise me you won't make a scene."

"I won't," I promised. "I only need to talk to him."

"I understand. This way."

She led me down a long, dim hallway lined with closed doors. I couldn't hear much thanks to the music, but there were definitely noises coming from a few. Toward the end she stopped in front of a door labeled with the number six.

"He's in there. Paid in cash to have the room all night." She looked at me with sympathy. "Good luck. For what it's worth, you're too gorgeous to let a guy bring you down. Even in that enormous coat." She chuckled and started back the way we came.

I leaned with my back against the door, taking it all in. The entire night seemed like some kind of alternate universe with every step leading me up to this moment.

I wanted to call Jamie so badly. If only to hear his voice urge me that I could do this. I let myself think of all the years with Scooter, every anniversary, every holiday, all the times he'd told me he loved me. He didn't know what love was. All he knew was how to take and how to pretend.

I lifted my chin high and pounded on the door with a closed fist. I didn't stop banging until a woman cracked it open and peeked her head out. I couldn't see much in the dim light, but she looked older than me, maybe ten years, and she had light hair hanging on either side of her heavily made-up face.

"What is it? We're all paid up already." She grinned as she took me in. "Unless you're here to join the party?"

I gave her my most lascivious smile. "I am. I heard it was a bachelor party and wanted in."

"I don't know nothing about a bachelor party, but I'm always down for another plaything." Her voice came out like a raspy purr, and she opened the door to let me inside.

The small room had a huge bed taking up the entire center and there were mirrors on every wall. Scooter was nude and blindfolded in the middle of the bed.

"Baby, who is it?" he groaned.

Every nerve ending in my body lit on fire. The woman walked toward the edge of the bed and sat beside him, then ran her fingertips up his abdomen.

"It's a special surprise. You're in for the night of your life."

She wasn't wrong about that. I glanced around the room and spotted a riding crop on a counter in the corner among a plethora of other toys. I grabbed it and squeezed the faux leather handle hard.

"God, baby. I'm so fucking hard. Come and suck my cock," Scooter groaned and bucked his hips off the bed.

I waited until I reached the end of the bed to speak. The woman watched me curiously while she toyed with Scooter's nipple. Without saying a word,

I raised the crop and swung it down on his dick with all my strength. He cried out in pain, grabbing his area with one hand and yanking the mask off with the other. The woman scrambled to her feet and backed against the wall.

"What the fuc—" he started. "Penny?"

Realization shone on his face as he took me in, still curled in a ball from my dick assault. I lifted the crop again.

"Hello, Scooter. Sorry to interrupt your lovely Christmas Eve." I landed the crop along his thigh.

At that point, the woman looked between us and grabbed her robe.

"I'll wait outside," she said.

Good idea.

"What the hell, Scooter? How could you do this? We're supposed to get married tomorrow." I raised the crop again, but he bolted up and caught it in his fist.

"Shit... I'm sorry. I'm so sorry, Pen. You weren't supposed to know." He tossed the crop to the floor and walked toward me. I backed away. If he touched me, I'd find something worse than a crop to whack him with.

"Stop. I don't want you to put another finger on me ever again," I said.

He held his hands up in surrender and stepped toward the side of the room to grab his boxers.

"What can I do to make this right?"

I laughed, a dry sardonic laugh that shook my whole torso.

"This was the tip of the iceberg. We've been done for a long time. It just took me years to figure it out."

"We're not done. Let's fix this, Pen. Come on, we've been together for ten years. Don't throw it all away."

I walked backward, not stopping until I hit the door.

"You threw it away, not me. You and your family have treated me like garbage for years, and now I find out, after everything, that you've been cheating on me? You're absolutely delusional if you think I'd marry you now."

"It was Russ. He made me come here. Ask Trish, she'll tell you." I laughed again.

"I already talked to Trish, and she told me plenty. We're done. Maybe that one out there will fall for your bullshit, but I sincerely hope not, for her sake."

I pulled the door open to an empty hallway. Before I stepped out, I turned because there was one last thing I wanted to get off my chest.

"Not that you deserve to know, but you'll find out anyway. I'm in love with someone else. Before you ask, no, I never slept with him, but we kissed. And to think, I felt guilty all day about a kiss when you've been screwing other women for God knows how long."

He pulled a hand through his hair. "Who is it? I'll fucking kill him."

"Goodbye, Cootie. Merry Christmas."

I shut the door in his bewildered face and stormed through the bar, giving a little wave to Scooter's special friend on the way out.

Chapter 10

DECEMBER 25TH

I woke up in my bed still dressed in my clothes from the previous night and clutching Jamie's notebook. Memories of the night replayed in my head, and none of them seemed real. Not Jamie's gift with his beautiful words, not Scooter and the club, and especially not the way I handled everything. Did I really whack Scooter's crotch with a riding crop? I'd be lying if I said I didn't enjoy making him suffer the teeniest bit.

I rolled over to find my phone discarded on my nightstand. When I'd gotten home last night in a daze of disbelief, the adrenaline high I'd been riding finally came crashing down. I remembered pulling my phone out and looking at Jamie's text thread. There were so many things I wanted to say that I couldn't decide what to write first. Sleep took me under before I strung together coherent thoughts to send to him. The screen was dark from a dead battery so I pulled my cord from the crack between the bed and table and plugged it in, holding my breath at what kind of messages would await me.

I needed to call my father as soon as possible. He was probably getting ready for a ceremony that would never happen. I flipped over and buried my face in my pillow. Hopefully, Barbara did what she did best and spread the news to all the other wedding guests. She invited them to begin with, so I assumed she started making calls first thing this morning. How would those conversations go? I'd love to be a fly on the wall when Scooter faced his mother today. Although, her little Cootie would always be perfect no matter what he did.

My phone came to life, beeping again and again. Rolling back over, I pulled the cord as taut as it would go and swiped it open. Messages popped up on the home screen, some were from wedding guests I barely knew saying how upset they were about the wedding. I laughed at the nerve of those people. Trish's name caught my eye, but I swiped it away. She's already said everything she needed to say last night. Then I caught Scooter's name. I swiped it open and read it with narrowed eyes.

Scooter: *I'm so sorry Pen. I can't lose you.*

Maybe he should have thought about that years ago.

Scooter: *Who kissed you? I deserve to know.*

Shaking my head, I swiped away from his messages. *He deserved to know?* Wow. There were no words for the lack of self-awareness that man possessed.

I scrolled to Jamie's contact and stared at the photo bubble above his name. His mouth pulled wide with a grin and his eyes gleamed. Heat flooded my face, thinking about the time I snapped it in the breakroom.

A plan formed in my mind, but first I had to call my father and break the news.

An hour later, I pulled into the driveway of my childhood home. My dad had set up the three-foot plastic Santa and reindeer on the front lawn and wrapped the entryway in colored lights like he always did every year since I'd been born. So much was the same, but even more had changed since my dad married Darlene five years ago. She'd planted roses along the side of the house, now dormant and covered in snow. Inside, she'd added so many small touches here and there over the years that the last time I visited I hardly recognized the place as the same space my mom used to call her home.

I didn't hold it against Darlene. She was a nice woman, and my dad loved her. It'd just been difficult to watch my mother's footprint get erased bit by bit.

My father opened the door, dressed in the same red sweater he wore every Christmas. A Santa hat sat on his head, which covered up most of his thinning salt and pepper hair. He reached his arms out, and I fell into them, craving his comforting scent and warmth.

"I'm so proud of you, angel," he murmured while patting my back. My father wasn't a soft man despite some of his goofy quirks. There'd only been three instances I'd seen him cry in my life. Once was when his mother passed away. I was a little girl and hardly knew what was going on. The second time was when we got the news that my mother's cancer had spread. Both of us were unable to sleep that night. I found him sitting alone on the back deck with a glass of whiskey in his hand and tears streaming down his cheeks. He never cried at Mom's funeral although I'm sure he did in private. The third time I saw him shed tears was when he spoke his wedding vows to Darlene in our small church in front of close friends and family.

He squeezed my shoulders with gentle care and spoke softly. "It'll be okay, I promise."

My head was heavy against his chest as the weight of what I'd avoided sunk in. But I nodded, knowing in my heart that he was right. I would be okay.

Darlene welcomed me with a warm hug and a large cup of cinnamon coffee. I sipped it and willed it to awaken my mind for what I needed to do.

Jason and his boyfriend, Kai, thrust wrapped gifts at me as soon as I sat down.

"Kai and I saw this in this adorable little bookshop in the city, and I had to get it for you." His handsome face morphed into a grin as he watched me open the wrapping with childlike amusement.

I tore off the paper to find a book titled *How to Publish Your First Novel*. Without saying a word, I pulled him into a hug. Someone else believed in me. I was so touched that I didn't know what to say other than, "Thank you. I love it."

Kai sipped from his giant mug and smiled. "When you have your manuscript ready, let me know. I have a few friends in publishing that would be willing to take a look."

"That would be amazing," I said.

We sat around the tree eating baked goods and opening gifts. I felt terrible that I hadn't brought any of the gifts I'd gotten for them. As soon as I heard my father's soothing voice telling me to come over, I went into autopilot and got in my car to drive directly here.

Once gifts were opened, Darlene turned on *A Christmas Story* and we fell into a companionable silence. They hadn't brought up Scooter or the wedding since I walked through the door and I was grateful. Sitting with my family for even a short amount of time gave me some semblance of normalcy before I had to deal with the aftermath of my canceled wedding.

I excused myself and went upstairs to my old bedroom. They'd turned it into a guest room a few years ago by exchanging my purple polka-dotted duvet for a neutral pale green set and swapping my posters of Jane Austen and Shakespeare quotes for framed photos of birds and flowers.

My old desk still sat in the corner facing the window. It was the same spot I sat throughout my teenage years filling countless notebooks with stories and daydreaming about seeing my words in print one day. Right where I thought they'd be, I spotted my notebooks stacked neatly in a pile on the corner. I grabbed the first one off the top, inhaling the nostalgic scent of pencil scribblings on old paper. Some of these were filled with lengthy stories of far-off fantasy worlds where kick-ass heroines slay demons real and pretend. But more of them held my thoughts and dreams. They were day-to-day musings of a teenager whose life went from ordinary to tragic in a matter of months.

I ran my hand across the notebook's cover, fingering the half-peeled-off sunflower sticker I'd hastily slapped on in the center. This was the last notebook I wrote in at this desk. Maybe a reminder of what I'd gone through would strengthen me. Lord knows, I needed that.

December 15, 2014

I don't know why I even opened up this notebook to begin with. Writing things down won't change anything... it won't help her. This week has been awful. Nurses have been in and out, my father paced the floors, and I waited by her bedside, anxious that if I moved for even a second it would be her last. I should be with her now. But I couldn't breathe. Mom's comforting scent of baked cookies and the hints of coconut in her shampoo was gone. As hard as I tried to find it, all I could smell was a sickly-sweet odor and iron, so much iron. Even sticking my face into the Christmas tree in the living room wouldn't get the smell out of my nose.

I hate myself for feeling this way. But I needed a minute. Dad says that it won't be long now. I've never seen him this way, so small and sunken in. He's had enough coffee this month to clear an entire aisle in the supermarket.

As bad as it is at home, it's worse going out into town with all the Christmas cheer and the tourists in to ski and shop. Carols play everywhere you go. It all reminds me that beyond my four walls life is going on. People are joyful and celebrating. Maybe we'll get a blizzard or something so I'll have an excuse not to go out. Dad never lets me drive when the weather is bad.

Scooter's been coming by every day. He's been cool and all, but it does kind of bother me how he always avoids talking about Mom. I don't even know if he's capable of having a conversation about feelings. He always wants to make out even when I tell him I feel weird since my parents are right downstairs. We pretty much only talk about his classes at the community college and how his parents are going to buy him a new truck if he gets good grades. They wanted him to go to Penn State, but he didn't get in. I did, but I didn't tell him. There was no reason to rub it in. Plus, it's not like I'm going to go.

I know he's being patient with me. We've been together for a year and only had sex twice. I want to but also... I don't. It's weird I guess. Maybe if I had some friends to talk to, it would help, but all I have is this dumb notebook.

Crap. Dad is calling for me to come downstairs.

I closed the book to stop the memories from resurfacing. It had taken nine years but reading my words hadn't caused my chest to cave in or my gut to clench like someone had stabbed me with a jagged blade. Yes, I still felt sad for myself and sad for my dad and all the things we'd missed out on in our grief. The sadness was still there; I think it always would be, but another emotion pushed the sadness aside like a shield, pride. I could finally look my eighteen-year-old self in the face and say we're going to be okay. We took a long time to get there, but we did it.

That's exactly what I needed to remember.

Inside my desk drawer, I pulled out a fresh notebook with a shiny black cover. I opened it to the first crisp page and began to write.

This would be my favorite story yet.

The sky looked like smoldering charcoal as I put my pen aside and closed the notebook. Scents of roasted turkey and baked bread wafted upstairs, but as famished as I was, I needed to go. Once the thoughts living inside me made their way onto paper, there was no going back. I had to see Jamie.

I hurried downstairs, my notebook under my arm, and hugged my father.

"Angel? What's the hurry?" he asked with a mouth full of a crescent roll he snagged while Darlene's back was turned.

"I need to see a friend." I peeked into the kitchen where Darlene fretted around and Jason and Kai drank wine perched on stools at the island.

"Please tell them I'm sorry for skipping out before dinner. It smells amazing," I said, grabbing my coat with my free hand. "This is important."

"Of course, whatever you need." He kissed me on the cheek and patted my shoulder.

"Love you, Dad," I said, my chest filled with warmth. My family may be small, but it's filled with love and resilience.

"You too. Be careful out there. The roads will be icy." I smiled at my dad being a dad even though I'm a grown woman.

I realized I had one problem while I walked to my car on the slick sidewalk. I hadn't texted Jamie since the previous night, and I had no idea where he was.

Crap.

Once my car was idling with the heat turned on full blast, I pulled my phone out to send him a message.

Me: *Hey... can you talk?*

My fingers ached as I held them in front of the vents. The car took so damn long to warm up. I glanced at my phone in the cup holder, willing him to respond. The adrenaline that had coursed through me as I wrote at my desk minutes ago subsiding with each passing second. What was I expecting? He's probably hurt and thinking I married Scooter. Of course he's not staring at his phone to jump the moment I text him.

With nervous energy coursing through my bones, I backed out and headed toward the one place that reminded me of Jamie—the hotel.

I didn't know what drew me there other than some instinct that buzzed deep within me. Those walls held our story. Our years of friendship were built like a Lego house, one brick at a time. I couldn't go home, not with these feelings needing to be released. I was like a balloon ready to pop. My home, where Scooter had made his mark for almost a decade, was so far away from my heart that to walk through that door alone on Christmas might break me.

Instead of parking in the employee lot, I pulled into a vacant spot near the lobby doors. Melvin leaned against the podium shuffling through a clipboard stuffed with paper.

"Merry Christmas, Melvin," I said, which broke his trance. He nodded, barely sparing me a glance, and went back to whatever he was so intently reading. Chuckling low, I opened the door and took in the empty lobby. Those same carols played low through hidden speakers, reverberating off the walls. The beautiful Christmas tree shone brightly across the room while a roaring fire burned for no one to admire. The front desk sat empty. Gary had a skeleton crew working for the holiday. He only accepted volunteers and offered a hefty bonus.

The phone rang, and on instinct, I shuffled behind the counter and picked up.

"Thank you for calling The Ridge, this is Penny," I said, forcing my pitch to be chipper.

Emmy was on the line asking me to radio call maintenance for a heat check. She sounded as shocked to hear me at the desk as I was to hear her calling from a room. I grabbed the walkie talkie like radio that we used to relay messages to the crew and sent Emmy's request in. She wished me a Merry Christmas and I promised I'd fill her in another time.

As I hung up the receiver and turned, my breath caught in my throat. Jamie was there, resting against the back-office door. He looked about as exhausted as I felt with his disheveled hair and an unshaven face. Those hazel eyes burned into me, saying everything.

I stepped forward, tentatively at first, watching the subtle shift in his posture. He swiped his palm down his face, rubbing his widened eyes, but he didn't say a word until I was inches from him.

"Burke?" The plea in his voice was raw and filled with at least ten other questions. He let his gaze linger on my eyes as a warm tear spilled down my cheek. A tear for every word I'd ever left unsaid.

His thumb caressed my cheek, wiping the tears away. He let his palm linger on my face, splaying his fingers across my cheek, and his desperate plea burned into me.

"Jamie," I breathed and stepped closer so our bodies were flush against each other, then I placed my hand on top of his. His warmth seared into me, setting every nerve ending on fire. He smelled so damn good. I'd let his scent take up permanent residence inside me and never leave so I could carry it like a personal potpourri.

I thought about his gifts and the notebook and every beautiful word he bared from his heart. I thought of how brave he was for opening up to me even when he faced possible rejection. I didn't think I was that brave. But Jamie was. He was quietly confident and unconventionally handsome. Not only was he brave, but he knew what he wanted and wasn't afraid to show it. To take it. I slid my gaze up, locking him in with a heated stare and let my mouth linger so close to his that one tiny movement would have our lips touching. I dropped the notebook that was still under my arm and let it fall to the floor as I threaded my hands into his hair.

"Kiss me," I said, then closed my eyes and reveled in the feel of his lips landing on mine.

When he had kissed me in the car, I wasn't ready for what he had to give, but now I was more than ready. I wanted every piece he offered and, in turn, wanted to give those pieces of myself to him.

He backed me against the door, trapping me against his hard chest. I let my hands rove up and down his back as I pulled him closer and sucked his tongue into my mouth.

"Shit, Penny," he cursed low against my ear. "I've wanted to do this for so long."

"Me too."

Our mouths collided again, and I savored the taste of him. He tasted and smelled like the only place I wanted to be; like cinnamon, coffee, and home. His hands tangled in my already messy hair and drew me closer. Like he wanted to climb inside my skin. He nuzzled my neck and his rough stubble sent chills down my torso to my core.

I let my palm skim the length of his chest, digging into his Christmas sweater. I wanted to feel him so badly, his skin on mine with nothing in between us. With the press of his hard length against my stomach, I knew he wanted the same.

He sucked my earlobe into his mouth, nibbling and teasing me with his tongue.

A moan slipped from my lips. He paused, pulling back to embrace me with his gaze.

"God," he panted. "I've imagined what you'd sound like moaning, but fuck, Burke, hearing you moan with my mouth on your skin might stop my heart."

It was like we were being woken from an intense dream. We looked around and realized where we were. So many emotions played on Jamie's face: desperation, hope, fear. He was expecting me to say this was a mistake and leave again. But that wasn't going to happen ever again. I smoothed my palm across his face, drawing a finger down his warm lips before kissing him softly.

"Come on," I said, reaching down to grab the notebook and pulling him toward the computer. "I think room 205 is vacant."

He breathed a sigh of relief and followed me upstairs.

Chapter 11

DECEMBER 25TH

We ignored the questioning looks from a few passing guests. My mind was set on one thing—telling Jamie how I felt about him with my words *and* my body.

I'd forgotten what it felt like to be wanted so viscerally and to want someone else with a mix of heady exhilaration and knowing calm. Since I was finally being honest with myself, I had to admit that I'd never felt more than a flutter with Scooter. Even when we were first dating, it was never more than a teenage crush. With Jamie, I felt so much. It's been lying dormant, waiting for something to bring it to the surface.

I pulled him into the room, and he closed the door with his foot. The lights were off except for a small nightlight in the bathroom that sent a sliver of amber through the open door.

Alone, in the quiet of our room, something shifted in the air. There was still urgency, that was clear from my pounding pulse and heaving chest. But I owed it to him to tell him how I felt. I sat on the edge of the bed and patted the space beside me.

"Is this real?" he asked with a tremor in his voice. He sat beside me and took my face between his palms.

"Yes." I leaned against him, shoulder to shoulder. "I read the notebook. Jamie, I—"

He kissed me. His lips were so warm and his touch so gentle. My body melted for him. I pulled back enough to let myself get lost in his darkened gaze.

"I want this. Badly. But I need you to know Scooter and I are done. And yes, you helped show me the way, but this," I motioned between us, "this is my choice. I want you. I need you to know you're not some backup plan or rebound, okay? It's been over with him for a long time. It just took me until now to see it."

His tongue darted out to moisten his lips while he watched me intently. When I finished saying what I needed to say, he nodded while rubbing his palms against the fabric of his jeans. Before he spoke, I handed him the notebook.

"This is for you. I wrote it today. It's a new story, one that's been in the making for a long time."

He took it with a raised brow. "What is it?"

"The beginning of our story," I said. Joy washed over me as I watched him open the cover and take in my writing. I poured every messy thought into those pages, not nearly encompassing the depth of my feelings. They were raw, vulnerable, and entirely me. A smile played on his lips while I focused on his breathing in the quiet of the room. When he reached the last sentence and read those three little words that said everything, his eyes met mine.

"You do?" he asked.

"I do," I nodded, breaking into a grin.

"Come here," he said. He put the notebook down on the bed and pulled me into his lap. Chest to chest, face to face, our feelings were there with nowhere to hide. I trembled with nervous energy. "I'm so in love with you. My chest cracked in two when I thought you'd married him. I still can't believe this is real."

He pushed a loose strand behind my ear and kept his palm buried in my hair. My nerves were a sparking flame from his touch.

"I know. I'm so sorry. I—"

"You don't need to apologize or explain. You're here. This is real." His exhales were shallow. "You love me?"

"I love you, Jamie. I love you so much." Saying it felt like the easiest and most natural thing in the world. His hands sank deeper into my hair as he leaned closer.

"Say it again," he exhaled. Heat and hunger in his gaze.

"I love you."

"You're mine, Penny," he said with a rasp that sent fire straight to my core before he crashed his lips against mine. He consumed me with renewed urgency like he had shed an outer layer of skin and bared himself for the first time.

I needed more.

His stubble scratched my face with painful pleasure, and his fists wrapped around my loose hair, tangling tighter with each thrust of his tongue. I sucked his bottom lip, which pulled a deep rumble from his chest. Loving his response, I flicked my tongue against his, nice and slow.

"Your mouth is going to kill me, Burke," he growled when I moved to his neck.

He found the hem of my shirt and he pulled it off. I did the same to him, yanking his sweater above his head, needing to feel the warmth of his skin against mine.

His shoulders were wide with lean, corded muscles. I let my palms explore the planes of his bare chest, sprinkled with the perfect amount of dark hair. While I paid extra attention to his nipples, he undid my bra, freeing my breasts. I climbed off his lap to shimmy out of my pants and panties. I was ready for anything and everything with him.

He reclined on his elbows as he took me in with a darkened gaze.

"You're so beautiful. I always knew that, but God... you take my breath away," he groaned.

I'd never felt as sexy as I did standing bare before him. He made me feel desired and confident like I'd never felt before. Wetness pooled between my thighs as need pounded in my veins. I stepped back into him and trailed my hand down his chest to the button of his jeans. Seeing what I was doing, he helped pull them off along with his boxers.

He was thick and hard as I wrapped my hand around him and spread his dripping moisture from tip to base.

My movement was a storm like thunder and lightning exploding between us. Sucking and kissing and rubbing until we drew out curses and moans from each other.

"Lie back. I need my face between your legs like I need air to breathe." He hovered over me, making his way down the soft curves of my body until he reached my aching center.

"Please," I exhaled, ready to writhe against the sheets for relief. He held my hip with one hand, and I let my thighs open for him. His mouth settled over me, and he inhaled before hissing under his breath. He dipped down to swipe his tongue against my clit, slowly and lavishly.

"God—" It felt so good. Too good. My pulse raced and my chest heaved as I tried to buck against his face. He held me firmly and took his time savoring me in a slow rhythm.

I climbed higher and higher with each push of his tongue. My body was coiled tightly, ready to snap. He pushed a finger inside me and matched the rhythm of his tongue, delving faster and faster and pushing me right to the edge.

"I'm so close." I moaned. "Jamie."

He sucked me between his lips, and I fell over the edge, screaming his name as my orgasm rolled through me in a wave of euphoria.

"I think I found my new favorite activity." He smirked before he swiped my wetness from his lips with his tongue.

"I'll never object to that," I breathed while waves of aftershock still rolled through me. I reached for his cock, so hard and throbbing. "I want you inside me."

He sucked in a breath and pinned me with his heated gaze. "God, you're sexy. Always take what you want, Penny. From now on, I intend to give you everything."

"I'm on the pill," I said. "I want nothing between us."

He visibly trembled as he notched himself at my opening.

"I want this to be so good for you..." he hesitated. "But it's been a long time."

"It will be good for me," I kissed him. "Because it's you."

He sank into me and groaned against my neck. "Feels so good."

"Mmm," I answered and moved my hips to feel him deeper.

We rocked, clinging to each other, and grinding out our pleasure. I felt myself approaching the edge again.

Wrapping my legs around his back, I pulled him deeper until he reached that spot inside me that sent me pulsing. I dug my nails into his back to hold him while my muscles clenched. Sounds I never knew I could make came from deep in my throat.

Jamie lifted his head so we were eye to eye while he ground his hips, seeking his release. "I love you so much," he groaned. "You're so beautiful when you come." He rocked into me again with his eyes blazing as he came.

"Don't get up," I crooned, holding Jamie's collapsed frame against me. Nothing felt better than him being as close as he could be with nothing between us.

"I don't want to crush you." He chuckled, nuzzling my neck.

"You won't. You'd never hurt me." Saying it out loud made me realize that there was no doubt in my mind. He wouldn't hurt me.

"Never." He wrapped his arms around my back and rolled to the side still buried inside me. We stayed like that for what felt like hours, caressing each other and whispering feelings in the dark. We made love again slowly, reveling in each other's pleasure.

"It's never been like this for me before," I admitted. I rested my head against his chest, tangling my legs with his. "This intense."

He tipped my chin up, making sure I was looking into his eyes. I'd have to get used to how much he loved eye contact so direct that he took in every part of me.

"Me either. We were waiting for each other, I think." So earnest and thoughtful. Everything about him had my heart squeezing and had me praying this wasn't too good to be true. He kissed me again and sank his hand into my hair. "Merry Christmas, Penny."

"I forgot that it was Christmas. It seems like it was ages ago," I said with a small laugh against his lips. "Merry Christmas, Jamie." *My Jamie.*

"By the way, next year I'm rigging Secret Santa again. Can't have anyone else declaring their love for you through gifts." He laughed. "I'm thinking I'll go the Toby route and get you a creepy poster of babies playing the saxophone. I'm done trying hard now that I have you."

I pushed up on my elbows and shimmied my body so we were eye to eye. Jamie's unmistakable smirk spread across his face and was punctuated by a literal gleam in his eyes. I scrunched my nose at him and gave him a light smack on the arm.

"If you're going to go *The Office* route, I better be worth at least a handmade oven mitt, buddy. And that mitt better have your blood, sweat, and tears poured into it."

He held up his hands in surrender as he chuckled. "Okay, okay. I will learn how to knit just for you. But don't expect Phyllis quality."

"There's always the teapot," I smiled.

"You'll just have to wait and see."

As dawn approached, streaks of golden yellow cut through walls of grey illuminating the sheets of freshly fallen snow. For the first time, as I closed my eyes, wrapped in Jamie's warm embrace, the phrase wait and see sounded perfect.

Chapter 12

DECEMBER 24TH, ONE YEAR LATER

"Thank you for calling The Ridge, this is Penny." I rolled my eyes as soon as I heard Gary's voice on the other end of the line.

"Is this the world-famous Pennsylvania best-selling author Penny Burke? *The* Penny Burke?" Gary said in a terrible fake Scottish accent. I shook my head while suppressing a sigh.

"This is her. How can I help you, sir?" He loved when I played along with his games and, being that it was Christmas Eve and the day before my week off, I was feeling a bit more jolly than usual.

"Well, I need a room. A pack of dogs trampled through my house, and they stole my turkey. Damn things broke my one-of-a-kind leg lamp too. Then I almost shot my eye out! Me house is cursed."

He was clearly going with the plot of *The Christmas Story*. An hour ago it was *Die Hard* and before that *Gremlins*.

"Oh no," I deadpanned. "I'm sorry to say that we're fully booked, sir. Maybe you can try the Holiday Inn in Scranton."

"Can't. See, my cousin, Eddie, showed up in his RV and kidnapped my boss. Now I'm wanted by the FBI."

I searched my brain. This was a new one. Cousin Eddie? Then it came to me, *National Lampoon's Christmas Vacation*. He was really on a movie marathon this week. Someone needed to stop him. I let him ramble on the line for another few minutes while I texted Jamie.

> **Me:** *I have a bit of a situation.*

> **Jamie:** *I'm an expert in situations.*

I laughed, picturing him at home in the kitchen prepping for our Christmas Eve date night in. He practically made me come to work so he could surprise me with something. I hoped it was a baked good...

> **Me:** *Gary keeps calling, doing different accents and saying his life is the plot of a Christmas movie again. Today it's The Christmas Story and National Lampoons.*

> **Me:** *Rescue me. Pleaseeee?*

> **Jamie:** *I have an idea.*

"...and me wife overcooked the turkey. The thing started smoking as soon as I carved into it. Dry and chewy but still good...," he went on. "...that was before Uncle Lewis burned down me tree."

As I gave him an indifferent response, he suddenly, blissfully, went silent. *Jamie.*

"Excuse me, Miss Burke, but it seems that a magician with a magic hat wants to meet me outside to build a snowman. Gotta go."

The line went dead, and I laughed, grabbing my phone to thank Jamie.

Me: *You're brilliant. Magic hat?*

Jamie: *Yup. I only wish I had planned this sooner. Could have paid Calvin to go over there and make a bunch of snowmen before Gary came outside.*

Me: *Missed opportunity. There's always next year...*

Jamie: *Where's that empty notebook you had in the living room? I have so many ideas now.*

Me: *See you soon, xoxo*

With Gary occupied, I got through the rest of my shift without issue. The air was filled with anticipation, and for the first time since I was a teenager, I was excited about Christmas. Jamie and I were taking a week off, partly because of my first book release, which was happening next week but mostly to spend time with each other while we enjoyed a quiet holiday. We'd visit with my father and Darlene tomorrow morning and then video call with his family in the evening. Jamie's parents embraced me as part of their family by showering me with love and supporting us unconditionally. His brother has done nothing but razz him about waiting so long to tell me how he felt. I guess he had been pining about me to him for years.

I couldn't believe so much in my life had changed in a year. Scooter left the hotel shortly after I broke it off with him. Last I heard, he was living with his parents and selling used cars in Scranton. That first week after I found him, he tried as hard as he was capable of, which was essentially making fake promises and attempts at flattery. Jamie stood by my side as Scooter came to the house and packed up his stuff. He hadn't realized Jamie and I were together but neither of us cared. I only wanted him out. Cleansed from my life, so I could start my new chapter.

The chill of evening settled in as I pulled into my driveway. Jamie and I had decorated my front door with a fragrant wreath and strings of white lights last weekend and they called to me like a beacon in the darkness. As I pulled the door open, the most wonderful scents of roast turkey, garlic, fresh bread, and the lingering scent of sugar hit me. I followed the smells into the kitchen with my stomach rumbling and my mouth watering. The closer I got, the more I could make out Mariah Carey's "All I Want For Christmas Is You" playing on low volume from the kitchen.

Jamie stood with his back to me as he pulled something out of the oven. He wore dark sweatpants that hung low on his hips and hugged his butt in just the right way with his favorite green Elf-Dwight-shirt. His chestnut hair stood on end as disheveled as ever, dusted with flecks of flour.

"Smells amazing." He turned at the sound of my voice and the widest grin spread across his face. I walked over to him and planted a soft kiss on his lips. "You have a little bit of something right here," I said, swiping flour off his cheek with my thumb.

"Saving it for later." He pulled a chair out, ushering me to sit down with a kiss on the top of my head. We ate a delicious turkey dinner while chatting and laughing about our day.

"I'm so full. I don't think I can make it out of this chair," I groaned. "It was all so good. You're cooking dinner all the time from now on."

He leaned back in his chair with his eyes lit up. "I hope you saved room for dessert."

"Depends… what's for dessert?" I added a bit of innuendo to my tone even though I was too stuffed to move.

"I'll show you."

He hopped up and grabbed something from the fridge. I watched his long legs move fluidly in those booty-hugging sweats. Suddenly, I wasn't feeling too full to move after all. He came back and set sugar cookie dough and a tin of cookie cutters on the table in front of me.

"I thought we could make cookies and watch *The Office*. I know you and your mom used to make the cookie cutter ones and wanted to—"

I kissed him, sinking my hands into his hair. Wetness gathered in the corner of my eyes at his thoughtfulness.

"I love this. I love you." I said, pulling back to look at him. "Thank you."

We made cookies that turned out looking like circular blobs but tasted like sweet perfection and settled in the living room to cuddle under a blanket side by side. With the roaring fire, lit tree, and lingering scent of sugar cookies in the air, I felt like life couldn't get better than it was at that moment. Jamie wrapped his arm around my shoulder, pulled me into his chest and turned on our favorite show.

I think I made the right choice.

I didn't just think; I knew.

Acknowledgements

Thank you to all my readers, you're making it possible for me to do what I've dreamed of doing since I could hold a pencil. Every post you share or review you give helps to spread the word and I'm so grateful.

This book was 100% a passion project. *The Office* has been there with me through my best times and pulled me through the darkest swells of grief. Like any mega fan of the show, I'd always daydreamed about getting to read the teapot letter and that's when the idea for Penny and Jamie's story took shape. So thank you to *The Office*- these characters and their stories are as much a part of me as any flesh and blood person in my life.

I couldn't do what I love without the support of my husband and family. Thank you for your patience and endless love. Leah and Branden, my soul sisters, love you both and appreciate all that you do. Brittany, once again you've helped me create the best version of the story that lives in my head. I appreciate you. Kylie, thanks so much for the gorgeous cover. Lea, you rock. Thanks for being my much needed last set of eyes.

Thanks for stepping into the beautiful, ordinary world of Greyridge. I hope you loved it there and want to come back again soon. In the words of

Pam Beesly, *"There's a lot of beauty in ordinary things. Isn't that kind of the point?"*

About Author

Lauren lives in Phoenix, Arizona with her full chaotic family. When she's not crafting her next happily ever after, you can find her playing taxi to her teenagers, being pulled by her two large dogs, and when she's lucky reading with a cup of coffee.

Also by Lauren

Palm Cove Series

Fight For It

Fight For Her

 instagram.com/laurengreenebooks

www.ingramcontent.com/pod-product-compliance
Lightning Source LLC
Chambersburg PA
CBHW030234180626
46810CB00008B/3127